Monster Sandwiches

A Love Story

HEATH ECKSTINE

DEDICATION

To my dad Russell Lee Eckstine, 1947-2010.
Thank you for teaching me to move through the world with integrity.

To my sister Amy Rene Eckstine, 1974- 2020.
Thank you for teaching me how to fight.

To my wife, Christina Mae Eckstine.
Every day, when I think I couldn't possibly love you more,
you prove me wrong.

To my family and friends who have traveled through the nexus to bring us
back your name. I am in awe of your courage and want you to know that you
are loved.

"Stay warm. It's cold out there."
~ Random stranger who seems to understand more than they understand.

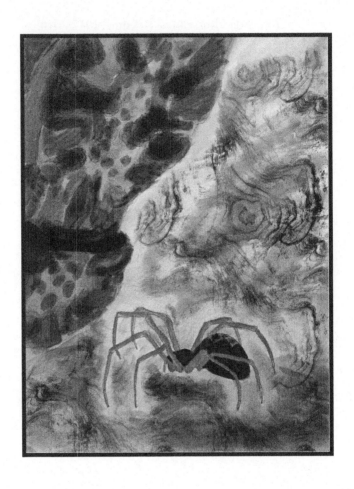

PREFACE

Earwigregalus Yohonamonstavitchnic should have felt more blessed than he did about his untraditional life next to the nexus. In a world filled with mud huts and roads paved with manure from goat-pulled carriages, he had magic. For as long as he could remember, every night after he fell asleep, he could be assured to wake up and discover gifts beyond the imaginations of his peers in the village. One of his favorites was a magical box that could be made to reveal stories from distant worlds, where aliens and robots battled on ships that sailed the sky.

Occasionally, new visions called VHS cassettes would be sent to accompany this box. There were machines that could wash his clothes and others that gave him water that cascaded over him in hot and cold. Stoves that worked without fire, fireplaces that pushed out hot air without fire, and black windows that produced the magic that powered all of these wonderful innovations. He even had cold air that blew into the massive hut his dad called a doublewide on hot summer days.

Earwigregalus and his father did not want for anything. Through them, the muddy, manure-scented village of Moon Valley got a little less dismal, at least when the villagers accepted their gifts.

Had they lived in the village, their good fortune may have invited thieves, rogues, or false friends but they did not live in the village. They lived next to the Nexus, a doorway between worlds, and behind that doorway lived a creature. Nobody had ever seen the full creature, just glimpses of slime-coated tendrils and spiked spider legs. Everyone had only ever seen enough of that creature to warn them away from the glowing blue-green hole in the field.

Earwigregalus wasn't afraid of this creature like the others, however. On the contrary, this creature gave him his name and so many other things. He should have and would have felt so much more blessed than he did but that *sacred name* the creature gave him, it was a mouthful.

CHAPTER 1

THE BOY WITH NO NAME

Earwigregalus pulled in his shoulders to slide through the glowing blue slit. There is no human experience short of being born that could compare with what happened next. The horizons of the world exploded around him. It was as though the world he had stepped out of, which had once seemed so large, was just a drop in the ocean. Even behind him, in the direction that he had just walked from, countless miles rolled on. Every inch of that journey was filled with a writhing mass of black and blue snot-covered tentacles, like that of an octopus, jagged leg bits, and fangs the size of trees, like those of a spider.

He lept back startled by its presence but there was nowhere he could stumble, fall or run to that wasn't part of the writhing, undulating, and scurrying mass.

"Earwigregalus," it cooed. The voice was soft like silk or something born of a gentle breeze, harmonic and beautiful. He knew that he shouldn't be scared. His father spoke of her benevolence and warned him not to insult her. She, the one who for many generations had been nothing but a source of eternal kindness and love to their family. Still, she was gigantic, slimy, toothy, and writhing all around. How could something that was so…whatever that was, be as wonderful as he had been told? Perhaps the villagers were right?

"The Nexus," he asked, after working up his courage. "Is something wrong? It has been shrinking. The gifts haven't been coming through. My dad said it always provides what we need and my dad needs medicine."

"The Nexus," she answered, "is dying. That part of me is dying. Do you know why?"

Earwig said nothing. He knew because he was a nexus keeper and all Nexus keepers understood more about how things worked as soon as they saw them. It was part of their gift. He also knew because he was told time and time again that his name was a sacred thing. He knew but he needed to hear it from grandma.

"I feed on love." She began to explain. "As long as there is someone on the other side of the door that loves me, then I can hold a door open into that world but some people have a hard time accepting me for who I am. This is why I gave you a name. In case you couldn't love me for who I am. I wove part of my soul into that name. Had you held that name dear to you, the nexus would be fine."

"I will keep my name then! I won't say I hate it anymore!"
Her tentacles recoiled and he understood that she had no patience for his bartering.

"It is too late for that. That is not love. Love is not the enjoyment of the gifts you are rewarded, nor the fear of consequences." Her tentacles relaxed. "I cannot force you to love me or your name. I want to help, but I cannot push anything out of that door anymore, not even you. It is dying. It is closing and once it closes, nothing will move either way."

"But my father..." Earwigregalus started to protest. A large wet slapping of tentacles and a strained shriek of grief silenced him.

"Don't speak to me of your father. He is one of the kindest souls to walk your world. Much like his father before him and his mother before him. I would have saved them all if I could but now only you can achieve that."

Earwigregalus felt hot tears streaming down his face. "How?"

"Easy," the monster responded. "Wonder my worlds. Find something of me in them and something in me that you can love. If you can do that, you will heal your door."

"How..." the word had just started in his mouth when her tentacles pulled away and her massive spider-like appendages hoisted the undulating mass of a central body thousands of feet into the air. He saw two shadows wiggling to produce a dancing silver strand of webbing behind her.

"Follow my thread, it will lead you to the doors. The rest is up to you."

"I don't know how much time he has!" Earwig could feel his blood getting hot. His dad was dying and all this glorified squid-spider could do was send him on some sort of wild chase. For what, adulation...to be loved, what hell did she think...?

"Then hurry!" Her voice shattered his thoughts. Her legs rose into the air further than Earwigregalus could see, latching onto some invisible distant edifice before pulling the rest of her body skyward. Somehow, her massive visage shrank into infinity, leaving nothing behind but the thread for him to follow.

Chapter 2

Sam and the Nexus

Our story really begins nine hundred, ninety-nine years and some odd months before the fateful day when Earwigregalus, in anger, belted out those momentous words and collapsed the Nexus. It began with a homeless beggar named Sam, running from the king's guards.

One might expect the world to look much different after so much time had passed. It didn't. The villagers still lived in mud huts beneath the shadow of a giant castle that ascended the edge of the Baraboo Mountains. There were carts pulled by goats on roads paved with straw and goat poop. It still smelled just as rank.

Even the rift looked much the same as it did after Earwigregalus cursed his name. It was a thin blue slit floating two feet off the ground, it could be seen from the north. The side of the slit that faced the castle appeared almost wide enough to climb into and somewhat round, between. However, if you were to walk between the north and west-facing sides of the slit, the shape of it would vary between orbs, cubes, and spiky balls of light. If you were to stand on the south or east sides of this tear in reality you would see nothing. From those angles, it just wasn't there.

Those features made people just as nervous back then as they do now. Add to that, the fact that everyone knew a monster inhabited that impossibility. One that so defied everything people understood about nature and you would see why only the desperate or the foolish would ever dare wander near the nexus.

"A loaf of bread, a loaf of bread, they'll take my head for a loaf of bread," Sam sang. "Not today, old man." He reassured himself, stopping at the gap. "Not today." He swallowed hard, singing again in his strained voice. "A loaf of bread. A loaf of bread..." The bread in his injured right hand was torn, caked in dust from the road, and to almost anyone else would be inedible but he was hungry, so hungry.

Sam didn't think of himself as a thief. Not like the king or the villagers or everyone else thought he was. He would haul water and hay to their goats at night, he would shovel out stalls when nobody was looking. He would pay it back, if he survived the night, just as he had paid back countless other scraps of food. "My theft isn't the crime. Me being alive, that's what the real crime is. Dammit if I just had the chance, I could be useful in the world. If I just had a chance."

Sam was used to talking to himself. He remembered ages past when his fortune was different and he had lots of people he talked to. Men talked to him about hunting. Women talked to him about men. Both of those things bored him. Children, even though they sometimes talked too much, had listened to him as he told them stories from his life as a traveling merchant.

These days nobody talked to him, men looked away when crossing his path. Women ushered their children to the other side of the street, again turning their heads to avoid catching his gaze. They didn't recognize the once successful man who fell from favor after being robbed himself. His luck just got worse and worse until it was nonexistent. He lost his hut, his goat, and what little of his wares remained. With nothing to sell and nowhere to live and afraid of starving to death in the cold, he stole his first pie from a window. That night he returned to the owner's house and pulled all of the weeds from their garden.

Several days later he stole fish from a fishmonger and again fixed all of their nets in the dead of night. What he thought was a short-term means to an end somehow became his destiny. A couple of the villagers took pity on him and left scraps on tables in their yards on occasion. Most of them did not and chased him away or shouted for the guards.

So it was this man who didn't see himself as a thief, became a thief to everyone else and it was decreed by the king that if he were to be caught he should be executed on sight. There was even a reward for the person who could take his head, but it wasn't very much. Three coins. His life was worth less than a loaf of bread.

So it happened that Sam ran to the one place where he knew he wouldn't be followed. The weird blue hole, in reality, he had once seen swallow a huge incoherent mass of indescribable horror. "If you're in here monster, and you don't eat me, I'd like that very much! We can break some bread. I'm afraid I dropped it in poo but I'll eat the bad bits and you can eat the good."

His hand touched the edge of the light. Thundering footprints from horses drew closer and he could start to see the outlines of guards firing crossbows and raising their swords.

Sam cursed. He had been raised better but sometimes how you were raised has no bearing on the words coming out of your mouth. He looked down, afraid to look forward to the horrors in the nexus or back to the horrors of the guards, and it was then that he noticed a large spider trapped beneath his feet.

"Sorry little fellow, I hope I didn't hurt you." Sam scooped it up. "You better come with me or those battle goats will squish you flat."

"Stop so we can kill you," a deep voice bellowed out from a barrel-chested man on top of the largest horse he had ever seen in his life.

"Don't worry," Sam said to the spider. "They're talking to me, not you. I have a plan but I'm afraid it's not the smartest plan." He reached his spider-bearing arm into the rift. He felt the little legs scurry off of him and onto some unknown surface. He cursed again. He wanted to move but couldn't. He wanted to scream but just stood there crying. He had made it to his forties, a long life by any standards but today was his last day and he knew it. The bolts were crashing all around. He could smell the dust from the road mixed with sweat and horse farts and hear the clanking of armor but he couldn't for the life of him, move.

Today was his day to die. He was going to die over a loaf of bread and the person who killed him would be doing it for no more than three pieces of bread. Maybe it was for the best. The world had turned ugly and mean. At some point in his life people just quit caring for one another and if that was the way the world was going to turn maybe leaving this world would be a mercy.

And then it happened. Something unseen: a giant blue-black tentacle shot out from the nexus enveloping him and pulling him inward.

"Welp, he's dead, might as well go back and finish our reports." Someone called out from the other side and just like that all of the noise and screaming and confusion gave way to silence.

Sam's eyes were still closed when a soft female voice whispered. "I eat neither bread nor people. I require a rarer form of nourishment."

When he opened his eyes there was a moment of shock and terror. The creature before him had blue-black tentacles like that of an octopus and giant lanky spider legs set between each of those tentacles. Two huge and no doubt venomous fangs loomed in front of a beak filled with toothy outgrowths like that of a lamprey.

It was, at first sight, the most horrific thing he could imagine, but its voice was kind. The spider he had just saved crawled along the tentacle closest to him, completely unalarmed. She continued, "For today, I have already been fed," the monster added

As far as he could see the floor was sheets of glowing blue webbing. The wall behind him where he assumed that he entered was composed of glowing silver-blue webbing that shot up to the sky and outward in each direction where it appeared to go on forever, just like the monster..

A small eternity plodded by before Sam, who was the chattiest person in the kingdom, could find the words he was looking for. "I reckon neither of us is suited to be judged based on our appearance. Thank you."

"They called you a thief?" The creature said in the form of a question.

"I don't think myself a thief," Sam answered honestly. "I pay everything back, however I can. A man has to eat though. I was a merchant once."

"Regardless, you have passed the test." One of her tentacles motioned toward the spider.

Sam understood what it meant right away. It was the simple fact that he couldn't stand to see an innocent creature get trampled and killed that stopped him from meeting the same fate.

"That creature is a part of me. As are all spiders, mushrooms, octopi, and weeds in the water. They are connected to threads of me that are wired through spaces in the world that you cannot see, a fourth spatial dimension."

"I'm not sure I understand what that means," Sam responded.

"It means, I am so much larger than you can see or even comprehend," answered the beast.

"No offense," Sam replied but from what I can see, you're really damn big!" He could feel her laughter and warmth filling him with comfort that he hadn't known in years.

"I like you," Sam admitted.

"I like you too, Sam Yohonamonstavitchnic. I have watched you for quite a long time now. I needed to be sure about what I suspected, so I tested you and you passed. What is it that you want or need most?" The monster asked.

"I don't need much," Sam said. "A little food. Some safety. I'd like to make my way in this world without worrying about the king trying to get me kilt. I wish people saw me for who I am and not just some damn thief and maybe a friend or two."

"I chose well then Sam. It will take some time and it might get worse before it gets better but you and your family shall have all of those things. I'll need you to do some things for me. You can earn your way."

"How?" his life had been hard. He couldn't imagine that the nice things he had asked for would ever come to pass. He couldn't imagine it was within his ability to ever be of any use to people, let alone a monster with threads that wrapped around the world.

"I am tied to this place Sam, but I have a very specific purpose and I am in need of a merchant. I will bestow gifts upon you, which you can deliver.

I will need you to make your home near the nexus. My hands are either too gentle to move these gifts or too fierce to move them. That is the easy part."

"The hard part then?" Sam asked.

"You will one day have children. It doesn't matter if they are your blood or not. I will have you take them to me to receive a special name. A name tied to a piece of my soul. You and your children's children forever after shall receive their names from me. Teach them to love their names and themselves. Teach them to lead lives without wanting too much, so they can be proud of who they are. Those sacred names will contain a piece of my soul and might not always be so easy to bear but if they can love themselves in the process, then they will love something of me. Love is my sustenance. It is all that I require to survive. This will be harder than it sounds. In return, they will have my protection, food, comfort, and purpose. Is this amenable to you?"

"I can really have children? At my age, you could do that?" There were tears in his eyes. "Yes, I'll do it. Yes, yes!"

"Now, about this king, I suspect when he finds you alive he will come after you. When he sees your wares, he will want what you have. It may be scary but I promise you, not one blade or bolt will touch you. He will send more and more troops and you will bring them to me and eventually you will help bring the king himself to me. I have a purpose for him as well."

"That sounds like the hard part," Sam replied.

"It is the inevitable part. It is the cost of staying alive when someone like that has other plans. I have seen his heart too. It is not like yours. Not entirely lost but not good. I will give him a curse wrapped as a gift and a gift which looks like a curse and he alone will see just how big I am."

"Hold on, hold on," Sam interjected. I admit he's not the nicest man but I don't want to see nobody get hurt or killed. Not on my behalf. I mean, I did steal that stuff. I broke the law and…"

"Don't worry Sam. I promise not to kill or injure anyone myself. I am a teacher and dead students don't learn much."

"Your wording seems pretty specific," Sam said as though he was asking a question.

"You are right. I will not lie to you. Feelings will get hurt," the monster warned. "I am an Eldritch Kindness. It is not in my nature to hurt others but sometimes that is what is required to heal them."

"Okay. then." Sam replied

"For the next thousand years, every mushroom in your kingdom will be edible and they will be more than abundant. Let the people know this and nobody will die for want of food."

"After that," Sam asked.

"You know how I explained that I move through spaces that you cannot understand?" The creature didn't give Sam the time to answer. "Time and space are connected. I can form myself into the shape of your space and time so that you may understand me but I am so large that parts of me wind through time itself. To me, forever is all at once. Some of what will happen, for me, has already happened. And some of it… let's just say that I always hope for the best. Sleep now, when you wake up the world will be different."

Sam had been talking for so long that he didn't even realize how he had curled up into the creature's tentacles. As she spoke, his eyes closed. The night passed in a blur and he woke up from the strangest dream. He had dreamed about everything the creature said about his descendants thousands of years from now and a poisonous mushroom.

He woke up with a start, trying to wrap his mind around the dream but every time his brain seemed to touch one place in that dream, it was as though everything else changed. Soon the entirety of the dream slipped away. He didn't even recognize that he was no longer in the nexus but in some sort of a house. Not a hut made of stone and mud like all of the others but a long straight walled rectangular building with wood-like walls, solid see-through windows, and a steel-like exterior. His brain had changed too, because as he looked about the multitude of wonders that he could never have even imagined and he found that he understood just what they were and how they worked.

There was what appeared to be some sort of fireplace blowing warm air. There was a box in the wall that could blow cold air. There were levers that when flicked, made lights turn off or on depending on whether they were up or down and ivory-like squares in the walls with three holes in them that looked a little like a face.

A small black box had a rope that connected to one of these ivory squares. It had a lever that when pushed down, got warm. He didn't know how it was that he was able to understand that the purpose of this box was to put bread into. There was another box that would heat up food and he seemed to know how it worked as well. Outside there were white squares with black rectangles in the center. He knew that they turned warmth from the sun into the magic that made the things in his house operate. He soon learned about his toilet, his sink, and the many other technologies he now possessed. He was the richest man in the world.

CHAPTER 3

GIFTS

Sam would have assumed that he had died had the world outside not reeked of goat manure. It was the foundation of his next big surprise as he exited the doublewide.

Goats! There were goats outside his door. A team of six silver wethers, each as big as a horse, stood watching the door almost in anticipation of Sam's arrival. Their shining black harnesses glistened under a fresh coat of oil connecting them to an impressive black carriage.

Instead of wood and iron, the wheels of the carriage were thin silver surrounded by black, and Sam's new brain told him that they were filled with air and would be lighter and easier for the goats to pull. Behind the two seats in the front of the cart were stacks upon stacks of panels, which used the magic of the sun, and stacks of batteries and lamps that worked without oil.

"To town then," Sam told his lead goat. It answered with a bleat.

There wasn't enough for everyone yet and he still owed a few people for the food he had stolen. The people who took pity on him and left food scraps out hoping he would steal them. The people who chased him off before he could perform acts of redemption, and the king.

.

As he made his way to the village he noticed a new slightly sweet smell coming from the trees around him. Long white mushrooms that looked like icicles were growing in bunches on most of the trees. "Food," he thought. "Once they know what it is nobody will go hungry, not for a thousand years." He collected several large bunches to bring to the bridge side encampments and ragged places that he was once forced to hide in, for the people he owed a different sort of debt to, but first to town.

It didn't take long for people to notice him coming.

"What the hell did you steal now Sam?" someone shouted. The king is already after your head!" He saw the same turned heads, the same rejected glances, with a few sympathetic but pity-filled glances. Everything had changed and yet nothing had changed.

"I didn't steal this. These are gifts, not for me, for you. It's magic from the nexus!" Nothing had changed. They hated him, they pitied him and they dismissed him. He was bringing them magic but all they saw was a thief.

So he stopped in the square not fifty feet away from two guards that were preoccupied with mugs of ale and began assembling the magic. The first thing he pulled out were candles that worked without flame. This caught some glances.

The next bits of magic he discovered were called fireworks and matches. When massive booms made sparks dance across the sky, the whole town began to gather around.

"Please, please let me pay you back. I don't have enough for everyone but there will be more tomorrow!" He passed out lamp after lamp and solar panel after solar panel until his cart was almost bare.

Sam signaled a guard, "Bring this to the king" he said. Sam lifted one of his lamps but paused and almost dropped it as a giant sword flew through his neck without hitting anything. The intended executioner dropped his weapon on the muddy ground. His eyes grew wide, his mouth fell slack and after what seemed like forever he turned and ran away faster than Sam had ever seen another man run.

One of the remaining guards took the setup, not knowing how to respond. Give this to the king, Tell him it's from Sam and I will have more for him tomorrow. My benefactor desperately wants an audience with him but I'm afraid my benefactor is unable to travel much."

The guard seemed sheepish. "I didn't want us to catch up with you Sam. It's just our job. I didn't mean for you to die…"

"I have no hard feelings," Sam interjected.

"But I saw you die. I saw that giant tentacle squish you into nothing!"

"Honestly." Sam said, "I've never felt better."

"But the monster!" The guard protested.

"That's not a monster," Sam retorted. "I didn't catch her name but she is perfectly lovely, once you get past all the fangs and tentacles. She's my benefactor. She's helping me put things right with folks and she wants an audience with the king. Please bring him these gifts and tell him that. Tell him I'll bring him more, so much more because I know that I've been a pain in his butt but he really does have to stop trying to have me killed. It's rude."

"I'll tell him but I don't see this going well for you Sam."

"I reckon," Sam said. "That it is going to go, how it is going to go. Now if you'll excuse me I'm off to go show my friends from the rough places that all of the mushrooms in the kingdom are now edible so nobody will need to steal ever again. I'm kind of over the king murdering my friends."

Chapter 4

A Message for the King

Jon Denim arrived at the castle bearing the strange gifts and the message several minutes later to find King Henesy Blauers pacing back and forth in the courtyard muttering to himself about the fungus everywhere.

Several guards tried to stop him. "He's in a real rutty mood today, Jon. If you talk to him about a thief now, it'll be the last thing you do."

"Why?" Jon asked wondering what could have put him in such a mood.

The guards continued, "The guillotine rotted through, the nooses all snapped and the sword he drew in desperation fell apart in his hands."

Jon shook his head, "I just saw something myself. I don't think I have much of a choice," he pressed forward.

"You there, guard?!" The king addressed him. "Is your sword still working?

"Aye," Jon answered, setting the contraption Sam had given him down in the yard instead. He set it up and turned the knob, causing the light to turn on.

"Fascinating!" King Henesy said, turning his attention away from the man whose head he had shackled to a stock.

"It's for you. It takes magic from the sun and stores it in this box so when it's dark it can be shined out from this…. I don't know what to call it, a bulb perhaps."

"That's really neat, don't you agree?" Henesy asked the condemned man.

"Yes. I'd like to have one of my own, one day," the man replied.

The king laughed. "Well, that's a nice thought but unfortunately, I have to kill you now, no offense."

"None taken, you're highness, but I do wish you would reconsider your options… " he paused as Henesy pulled the sword from Jon's sheath, clanking it against the ground hard to make sure it was solid.

Assured the weapon was fit for duty he swung hard and the sword seemed to melt around the condemned man's neck making contact with nothing before it clanked to the ground. The man breathed out in relief.

"Oh for the love of crap! Is nothing in this castle working today?!" Henesy bellowed.

" Your candle seems to be working fine." The condemned man offered. "Perhaps it's just not a good day to kill me, maybe try again tomorrow?"

"But I gave you your last meal," the king protested. What is the point of giving you your last meal if I just have to feed you again tomorrow to be humane?"

The stock fell off of the condemned man's neck. He looked up and shrugged.

"OK, at least the sword didn't break." Henesy sighed, "I need you to do me a favor, hold real still and I'm just going to sort of push this into your neck real slow like. That oughta do the trick."

"I'd prefer not to," the man said. The king towered above him pressing the blade to his spine so hard that it snapped and yet it left the man unharmed.

"Fine!" the king said with a heavy huff. "Just go home, the execution is ruined!"

"Thank you sir!" the condemned man answered. That's very kind!"
"Indeed," Henesy agreed. "It's quite magnanimous, but quit stealing!"

The king's attention now turned back to the device. "Where did you say you got this?"

"Well sir," Jon answered. "That thief that died yesterday. He didn't quite die. Apparently, the nexus monster is his friend now and it wants to meet you. It also would like you to um…" Jon's voice dropped an octave and pitched up all at the same time as he concluded, "quit executing."

The curse-filled rant that followed could be heard from the Nexus to the under-bridge encampments where Sam was at that time, enjoying a feast of mushrooms and explaining his strange tale to people that he hoped would now have the means to survive without having to steal.

CHAPTER 5

BEGINNINGS AND ENDINGS

One day turned into another, which turned into weeks, then months, and then years because unless you're a giant transdimensional spider-octopus that's just how time worked. In this process, everything changed but some things didn't.

The villagers all got used to luxuries like toilets, running water, electric lights, heaters, and air conditioners. Sam made friends with everyone from one end of the town to the other. It wasn't the gifts that changed people's opinions about Sam, it was how he toiled.

Though he woke up to fresh wonders every day, he could feel who needed the objects most. He didn't often feel that he needed anything. He cycled through the same three shirts and though he now owned a pair of shoes, he only owned one.

When people did get gifts from him it always seemed to be something they would soon desperately need. Moreover, he had an instinct about people.

He would find them, sad, lonely, grieving, and stop his cart for long enough to listen. A lot of their problems were things he couldn't change or help but he could listen.

Sometimes that small act of kindness was more than enough for the people he encountered to find their own solutions. Sometimes, nothing could help but at least people had a non-judgmental ear to vent upon. He didn't share any secrets he was told or talk about other people's business.

When he wasn't listening he talked about things like the seasons, the birds he saw, and how he had seen them in other kingdoms when it would have been winter here. He talked about books he had read and the antics of his goats. He warned the younger folks not to be in too much of a hurry to grow up because one day he was seven years old and then he took a nap and woke up as a thirty-five-year-old man, with a thirty-five-year-old man's responsibilities and a thirty-five-year-old man's knees. He added that was almost ten years ago. It would have been only five years ago but he took another nap. When it rained before he was done with deliveries, he would just smile through his eyes and say that it was time for him to bathe again anyhow.

The gifts helped people to open their eyes and see him but it was the act of seeing him that made it hard for them not to love Sam. The only person whose opinion didn't seem to change so abruptly was the king.

Every day Sam saved his final gifts to give to the guards for Henesy, always with the same message. "My benefactor wishes to meet King Henesy." The king sent guards after Sam but they couldn't draw their weapons and every time they pursued him something broke or the horses disobeyed. They were neither able to stop him from delivering gifts to the villagers nor to harm him. Once following that order became more trouble than it was worth, they just left him alone.

One of the two negative things that the villagers associated with Sam was that violence wouldn't work for anyone. While bugs could still bite and foxes kill every hen in a hen house, people were unable to swat those bugs or dispatch those foxes and when two people tried to square off they could never land a single blow, producing an often comedic show.

The other problem was that people still got old or sick and then died. Between the lack of violence and the onset of clean water and treated sewage, it wasn't a daily occurrence but that didn't matter to the people who had just lost a loved one at a time when miracles seemed commonplace. Much like the farmer who just lost all of their flock to a fox and then had any chance at vengeance thwarted by supernatural forces.

This was all very well by Henesy. Sam having a handful of detractors made the king's former opinions of him seem less evil. The low death rate and having most of the kingdom content helped him look competent, even if it had nothing to do with him. As the months piled on vexed by the presence of something that no power in his entire world could challenge, it helped his kingdom to prosper and made his reign for the first time ever, appear successful. Henesy decided to do the only thing he could do, nothing.

More months went by and he went from vexed to concerned about what the trade-off would be. Soon years went by and the presence of the beast went from concerning to tolerable. After all, everything was getting better and he still lacked the power to challenge the beast.

This is how he tolerated it. Instead of hunting down criminals and preparing his defenses against the threat of another kingdom deciding to lay siege to Moon Valley. He often took his wife Judith out for coffee in the mornings, walked with her in the rose gardens in the afternoons, or practiced archery with her. She always hit her target. He always missed.

They watched the stars every night. Judith would point out individual specks and call them by name while he imagined that it was an ocean they could swim in. He wanted to swim in them with his wife forever.

He fell in love with her again even though at his most ill-tempered, even when he was mad at her. He never had the ability to feel anything but love for Judith.

Henesy even tried to compose a poem about that feeling but couldn't find the words. Nevertheless, he read it to her, stumbling over his tongue. When he realized how bad it was feeling secretly hurt he tried to laugh it off but Judith stopped him with a kiss.

Judith joked, "Had I known the beast in the nexus would sweeten ya so, I would have paid it a visit myself years ago darling. Ya've always been a crass man but I knew that part of the real you was still around. I've always loved you for it."

One day Sam dropped off a cart full of heated blankets, a bassinet, and a walker at the castle and was met with the king himself.

"I have no heir, so why would I need this?" he asked.

To which Sam answered. "She says you will in about nine months. It seems not all of your arrows have missed their mark."

King Henesy's feelings about the creature seemed to shift again. In just a few years it went from vexing to concerning, to a feeling that was almost fondness.

"My benefactor does want to meet you, king. Can we be expecting you?"

The king who had a wild giddy look on his face embraced the former thief, kissing his brow. "That's a definite maybe, but probably not." the king answered. "Still, a baby, a baby..." he continued.

Sam pulled his hands away quickly as the king appeared to be drawing him into a dance. "You're a good man, Sam! A good man I tell you! Let no one tell you any different."

That night, Henesy had the castle chefs prepare a banquet for the entire town. They wrapped up the gifts he had received in decorative parchment all addressed to Judith. Every prisoner was even pardoned and released on the condition that they attended the event.

Judith regarded the occasion with deep suspicion. She had always been the soft heart of the kingdom. If the condemned were ever pardoned it was due to her whispering, "Come now dear," to the king as he raged. She just wasn't used to seeing her husband, smiling and dancing and talking even more sweetly than he did the night before.

Henesy however was intent on making the occasion perfect. "On the day we were betrothed. When you first met me. What did you think?"

"To be honest dear, on that day I saw someone bump into you and spill your ale. Your response frightened me a little, why?"

"Oh..," the king said, feeling a little uncertain. Judith saw that look in his eyes, that spark of worry, and the ten thousand weird examples of how he was trying to show his love, from the condemned men reciting sonnets to her to the kitchen staff cooking pumpernickel bread with lime zest.

"Aye, yes. I learned you have a temper but then I saw ye reading to the orphans and when my father fell ill, you sat with me all day while I grieved and paced. Yer far more than the brute I saw that day. We may have been forced to wed, but I couldn't have loved another man. Nor another man make me feel as loved as you do dear." She clasped his right hand between both of hers drawing it to her lips where she kissed it again and again before embracing it. "But why my king?"

"Well," the king replied. "I have an announcement. You're pregnant!"

Her face drew into another puzzle. "So soon," she laughed, then paused. "You know, that's not how those announcements are supposed to go, love. How could ya know?"

"Sam," the king answered. He snapped his fingers and one by one, more of his former prisoners came forward and presented the gifts.

Sam was right. Nine months from the day of the party, Prince Philip came into the world, with a healthy visage of innocence and kindness.

What Sam knew but didn't say was that not long after that Queen Judith found herself unable to eat. Within days she started to limp. Within a week she couldn't raise herself off of the bed. That night she struggled with even the slightest movement of her hands.

It was then, in the middle of the night, that an army of guards slammed their fists against Sam's door and announced that the king was ready to meet with the monster.

It was the king himself standing between the guards at the front of Sam's door. His face glowed white and sick with terror. He only spoke two words to Sam. "I'm ready," and didn't say another word as Sam led him through the moonlight into the heart of the nexus. It was not until he was facing the beast that he spoke more. Growing taller as the rage and grief seemed to pick him up off his feet. "Did you know?"

"Unfortunately, yes," the monster said. "I wish I didn't."

"Please," the king fell to his knees, placing his crown on the ground. "You can have my kingdom. You can have my soul. I will commit myself to be your willing slave but please I beg you, spare my love!"

"This was not my doing, and it is not in my power to prevent it. I wish we could have met on better terms"

"I know, I know, I know, I don't deserve it. I'm not worthy of any of your gifts. I have been terrible but please," his mind kept replaying the images of his life with her. It wasn't just sorrow or absence but guilt. He had led a selfish life and she had loved him regardless. She was always rubbing his back or his feet or saying soothing sweet words even as his temper flared to tempest and he repaid them with cruelty. "Let it be me. Why didn't you tell me? Why didn't you tell me?"

"Even you," the beast answered. "deserved some measure of comfort and joy. Had I let you know how it would end, it would have stolen the joy of your son's birth from you. You would have only seen the loss. To tell you would be cruel."

"But I love her, I love her so much and I never told her enough. I treated her like, like some possession. She needs to know, she needs to know. Dear god, please!"

"A god I am not but I know how you feel and so does she. If it will comfort you, your son will live to see an entire century pass. He will be healthy and strong and good for most of this life. Much of what you love in her, you will find in him. Please, be the father she knew you would be."

"But I love her, I love her! He protested, "Not her, please not her!"

"Go to her, tell her that." the monster interjected. "I will send you there. For there is not much time." A tentacle flashed before him and he was gone leaving Sam and two startled guards.

"Don't worry," Sam said looking back at them. "He'll be at the castle but you guys have to take the long way."

CHAPTER 6

POKIE

That was not the last knock at Sam's door that night. Just as he fell asleep for the second time there came another knock that ended that pitiful attempt at slumber. While it was the worst night of sleep he'd had since making his deal with the monster, it also represented the best night of sleep he would have for many years to follow. This time when he went to the door and flung it open shouting "What?" He only saw the faintest of shadows disappearing into the woods. Just as he was about to throw the door shut, a tiny squeak sent his gaze towards his feet. To a bundle of rags with a note.

"Please don't be mad. I am too young to have a baby, I can't give it the life it deserves, but I know you can. You're a good man Sam. I know you will take care of her better than I ever could."

A path of glowing blue mushrooms began sprouting from around the baby leading into the Nexus. "Really," Sam asked. "Now? My god I don't know what I'm doing!" As he scooped it up the baby laughed. "Don't get me wrong, you're about the cutest little pain in the butt I know. I just pray I don't break you." The baby laughed again.

"Listen you're new mom figure might seem big and scary but trust me she has the best heart of anyone I know, so don't get too taken aback by the tentacles and the fangs and the slime and all those legs. Just give her a chance."

The baby pooped, then laughed. "I'm going to have to clean that up. I don't know how to clean that up," Sam protested.

Sam followed the glowing marshmallow-scented mushrooms to the nexus, pausing at the gate as he pondered what it meant that he was about to hand this sweet little cooing child over to the giant tentacles of a beast and whether or not that made him a bad father. As of yet; however, the creature had yet to steer him wrong. On the other side of the slit, it was waiting towering like a mountain with two tentacles and two spider legs outstretched to greet the child.

"Don't worry Sam. Fatherhood suits you. It accepted the baby. raising it hundreds of feet into the air and peeling off the blankets while the spider limbs wrapped it in a new silk blanket, much the same way a real spider would wrap up a meal. The silk shined blue and the monster returned the baby to Sams' anxious waiting arms.

As she did, her words fell from Sam's lips, "Poecilotheria, Your name is Poecilotheria." He could see the beak raise up and down as the monster nodded in approval. He didn't say anything else, just accepted the baby and returned to his double-wide trailer house. There, as expected, he found a box filled with diapers, wipes, a bassinet, and toys. "Alright Pokie, (somehow he knew that the nickname was acceptable) let's get you cleaned up." Pocelatheria cooed again.

It didn't take long for Sam to find his way around being a father. Within a couple of years (that passed way too fast for his heart to accept) he was even able to sleep again. As the years went on, his partner in crime sprouted like a weed. It was weird how the most difficult parts of Pokie's childhood were the parts that he came to miss the most later on.

The other thing Sam found weird and unsettling was how the guards all continued to carry useless swords that they never drew on anyone for fear of them disintegrating. King Henesy took almost just as well to fatherhood and anyone who had not known him in the time of his campaign against thieves would almost have considered him a kind-hearted, albeit foul-mouthed soul.

It was a good time for Sam, and a good time for the monster which while already enormous, seemed to grow tenfold each week. Everything was better, everyone knew why and for all of the good it had done, almost everyone in the village had come to love the nexus and the monster inside.

Almost everyone. King Henesy, while not hating the monster, could not help but feel as though it could have done more to spare him the grief of having to watch his wife die in his arms. He had seen with his own eyes how much magic people now took for granted. With so much magic saturating the world, surely death did not have to be the inevitable conclusion of life.

The answer he knew was inside the monster. Not being able to execute thieves freed up a lot of time. He spent this time, when not doting upon his son, finding out everything he could about the Eldritch Kindness and immortality.

That was the good thing about being a king in a world with very few problems. He read every book in his library and found just the tiniest of scraps of outdated superstitious myth. The answers were not in any book from his realm but in a book delivered to him by Sam, from the kindness itself. It was almost as if it wanted him to know what it was, how to kill it, and how that would help him and all of his village achieve eternal immortality.

He read it cover-to-cover three times before locking the book in a chest, which was locked in a bigger chest, inside of a vault, in a locked room, which he kept guarded day and night by ten guards. He ordered them to keep everyone, including him, from ever seeing that book again.

As the years continued to pass he often wondered why he didn't just burn the damn evil book. As far as he knew violence against books wasn't frowned upon in the way violence against people was. He wanted to but he couldn't. Something about it affected him in a way that he couldn't understand.

Chapter 7

Dad Sandwiches

At age seven, Prince Philip happened upon a bakery while walking with his dad and begged to see inside, enchanted by the smells of wheat, caramelized sugar, the sawdust floor, and the multitude of mushrooms. It was there he decreed, "I will never be a king, dad."

"One day you will be though," Henesy answered his protest but Philip went on.

"No, this is what I want to do. I want to make sandwiches and feed people."

"It is a noble profession," Henesy responded, "but whether they know it or not people need someone to guide them. I have done the best I can but I have also made a lot of mistakes. When I'm gone it is a comfort to know that you will take my place."

"That's the problem, daddy. I can't take your place. You need to live forever." The king sighed and then shivered a little when he thought about the book.

"One day son, a long time from now I hope, my time will pass. If I tried to live forever, I wouldn't be me forever. What do you think would happen if we ate one of these sandwiches but instead of getting full our hunger only grew? What if the more we ate, the hungrier we got?

"Well then," Philip answered. "I'd start to look like you." He said rubbing his dad's stomach.

"Yeah, we'd get good and fat, but we'd eat all of the food and with nothing left to eat our hunger would be unbearable. This is how the world works. Life is a series of experiences and living them helps us to fill up and fill out but if we experience all of them or even too many of them, all of the joy, all of the stuff that makes life worthwhile would be empty. It's not right and it's not nice but that is how it works.

I hate death. It scares the crown right off my head. I spend a lot of time thinking about the things I still want to do and what people will remember about me when I'm gone. Will they remember me as a good king or will they remember when I thought I was a good king but I really wasn't? My one comfort is that my real legacy won't be my deeds but the fine young man who can carry on my name and be ten times the king I ever was."

"Dad," Philip interjected. "Can we just buy a damn sandwich now?"

"Yes, I'll make you one better young baker. Go talk to the master here and have him teach you how to cook. You go make us some king-worthy sandwiches and we'll get good and fat."

The baker, Mr. Bradly Morris, was a giant of a man. He was wide and tall with twinkling eyes and an easy laugh that came out every time Philip said something witty or inappropriate. He was more than happy to tutor young Philip in the culinary arts. Morris taught him about meat, in the time before when slaughtering an animal was easier. He had managed to pull it off a few times since the kindness settled in but every time he did it, he cried for days and everything he made with it tasted like sadness, so he learned how to season mushrooms instead. The flavor wasn't as deep or rich as it had been with meat but it beat serving people sad burgers with a snotty nose and tear-stained cheeks.

.

Philip liked him. He liked how he laughed and joked or how his words bumped into one another.

"Iana-willin-vegteren-is-jusa-way-da-worldis."

The back of Mr. Morris's shop was enormous compared to the five booths and counter in the front. Long tables covered in heaps of dough, more long tables with pots and pans, and six giant ovens shaped like igloos taller than Philip. They blasted the kitchen with a steady stream of hot smoky air.

"Made-em myself, I did. Ma pa taught me how to weave the willow-n cover the willow n mud. N then I had to keep the top of that mud wet fer nigh a month, lest it crack. It was all crumbly and weak but once I lit a fire in it, ya know what happened?" Mr. Morris smiled. "That mud turn to stone." He rapped his fingers against the top of one of the ovens making it clang.

"I always thought people were like that too. Lots of folks walkin around only doing what they have to do. They ain't never had no fire lit in them and ya might look at them and think they're all soft n brittle. But once a man finds what he loves and starts doin that. Nut'n in the world is gonna break him, not just men, women, even kids."

Mr. Morris turned to his long table pulling up one of the lumps of dough. "Smell this prince." There was an explosion of sweet, sour, and savory.

Philip's eyes lit up.

"It ain't nothing yet," Mr. Morris said with a sly smile. "This is the seed. This is my fire." He pulled a long forked iron bar off of the ceiling and lined it up with two holes on a pan, locking it into place before sliding it into the oven and lifting the fork at an angle to pull it free from the pan. "That was my fire, young prince. Here," he handed over the fork.

It took both of Philip's hands to hold the heavy fork in place. It took all of his strength and concentration to line it up with the holes on the next pan. Mr. Morris stood back, watching with a look on his face, as though he were figuring out a puzzle.

When the king first asked him to teach Philip, Mr. Morris had assumed that he would endure a one-day nightmare of washing extra dishes from a kid who wouldn't quit licking spoons, pans dented from the clanging

42

of utensils against them, and an endless barrage of questions that had nothing to do with baking.

Instead, Philip stood back. He watched with bright eyes. He asked how long to bake the bread, and how to know if the fire was too hot or too cold. He washed dishes on his own when he saw the baker doing it.

Mr. Morris showed Philip how to knead the bread, how to set it on the oven top to raise in the warmth, and how to smell when the dough had just enough of every ingredient. It took hours to prepare. Philip's hunger and anticipation doubled with every passing second but he would have to wait for another sixteen hours while the bread baked in low heat and steam rose up out of a kettle in the bottom of the oven.

It was well into the night when the first of the loaves were done. This was also when Henesy returned for his son. The baker had Philip and the king wait while he disappeared into the kitchen. He returned holding enormous half-loaf sandwiches topped with melted cheese, sprouts and three types of mushrooms.

"Well young prince this is a new recipe for me and since ya helped me make the bread. I'd like you to name them."

Philip dubbed them *Dad Sandwiches* in honor of his father and because they were huge, like the king. The flavor of the sandwiches was like a symphony in his mouth. There was sweet, salty, savory, and even a little sour, all playing their parts perfectly. Contracting in just the right portions and in just the right ways. Philip felt as though he might weep with joy.

"With your permission king," Bradly said. There was a seriousness in his voice that Philip had never seen. "I'd like to give the prince something that I ain't never shared with anyone. My pa passed it down to me. I don't wanna overstep my bounds but ya see, I never got the chance to make my own heir. It'd be a crime to let it die with me." There were tears in his eyes as Mr. Morris's hands darted into his pocket and pulled out a sheet of parchment engraved with a recipe. "May I?"

The king nodded. Mr. Morris's hands trembled as he pushed the parchment to Philip. Philip read the recipe, remembering his day and the smell.

"Dad. I made this today. This was the bread we were making." He turned the recipe to Henesys face but Henesy who was watching the baker's horrified expressions raced his hands to cover his own eyes.

"Those words are not meant for my eyes, son. This is like one of the sacred gifts. It is just for you and it comes with a responsibility. You must keep this secret until you are older like us and when you pass it on. You only pass it on to the right person to keep that secret bread alive, do you understand?"

Philip quickly folded the parchment and pushed it down in his pocket, his hands checking, again and again, to make sure that the recipe was safe. He then turned to Mr. Morris and hugged him, hoping to show that he understood how much the gift meant and how seriously he took the responsibility.

"I'd like ya ta come back and help me some more young prince. If that's ok with you and yer dad?"

"Can I?" the prince asked. Henesy nodded.

Within a month, Henesy would be looking forward to a new and improved dad sandwich. One for every time he took his crown off for the day. As it turns out, what Henesy thought was just going to be a phase or a childish fascination turned out to be Philip's greatest passion.

Philip returned to that shop every day, until one sad day seven years later. On that day, he opened the door to find the man that he thought of as a second father asleep in his chair, except Philip had never seen him asleep. Every day Mr. Morris raced the sun out of bed and won by hours. He retired after dark. If he wasn't tending to the fire, there was milling grain, washing dishes, sweeping, and dusting the flour off from every surface.

Philip's hand pressed firm on Mr. Morris's shoulder. "Get up, the day's half over. " He teased. It was something Mr. Morris often said to him because he showed up with the sun after half of the work was done.

"Mr. Morris?" He was cold, silent, unmoving, and unbreathing. "Quit pulling my leg. It's not funny." He could smell it in the air. The fires were all almost out. The bread had risen and was on the verge of going bad. A couple of loaves were already bad.

"GET UP!" A part of Philip knew. There was no point in shouting, or trying to pretend this was anything other than what it was. "GET UP! GET THE HELL UP! NOW, DO YOU HEAR....?" He couldn't shout anymore, He couldn't pretend. A part of his soul, a voice of constant love that he had known for half of his life was just gone.

His father later did his best to put this day into perspective. "I know this isn't easy to hear, but he was old and wasn't in the best of health when he was young. This was why he was so happy to teach you. He had no wife. He had no kids but because of you he still has a legacy."

A million other people would tell Philip how sorry they were. They would tell him that time would heal him, they would give him their most well-meaning unsolicited advice and he would accept it with a soft thank you but it didn't help, not really.

He had a wake in the courtyard of the castle like one that would be put on for royalty and everyone in the village came because everyone in the village loved Bradly Morris. They ate bread and laughed at stories from his past while sighing and crying. Then they stood around as he was lowered into the royal burial plot and none of this made Philip feel any better. There was a will and Philip found himself the sole heir to a building that hurt too much to enter, other than to keep the fires burning because he knew that's the way Mr. Morris would have had it.

He may have never baked another loaf but one day a goat cart pulled up to the cemetery.

"Philip," came the voice of the rift keeper's daughter. He had seen her with her dad in the bakery some mornings. He knew her face. He knew her name. That didn't make her any less of a stranger to him. He turned his eyes and betrayed all of the tears he was holding back. His lips parted but no words came out.

"I'm sorry you aren't on my route but I was just getting done and I saw you. I don't want to be a pest but, if you want to talk or not even talk, just someone to be with?"

His lips drew a half-hearted smile. "That's very kind."
More silence followed before Philip found his words again. "He gave me the shop. I knew it would happen. He didn't keep why he was teaching me a secret but I can't. When I walk into that place, he's everywhere. I can't do it. I can't and it makes me feel like a traitor."

Pokie clasped both her hands around Philips' trembling right hand.

"Even the oven that I made. The ugliest one and he insisted on using it every day." Philip continued. I can't stop thinking about him and still, I'm afraid I'll forget the details and lose him all over again."

Pokie's hand tightened. She wanted something better to say but was afraid that whatever she said was going to be the wrong thing.

Philips' lips parted again and this time words poured out. "This is what he wanted, hell it's what I wanted more than anything in the world. I never wanted anything to do with the throne. So why is it so hard for me to honor him?" As the words came out so did the tears. Philip found himself falling apart in front of this strange girl as she just stood there holding his hand with some stupid worried look on her face. He felt like she should have resented this show of tantrum but after a while, he was breathing again and telling her about playing chess over the course of months against the baker.

He told her about how Mr. Morris always greeted him with *"The day's half over"* no matter how many hours before the sun Philip arrived. Also about Mr. Morris sending him out to gather sticks and clay to make a new oven and telling him it was the best damn oven in here, even though it was small and lopsided.

He swallowed hard and asked her if she would walk with him. He had to tend to the fires but today he had to tend to something else, the legacy. She obliged. walking in silence as Philip led her to the bakery. Waiting inside as he started the fires. He offered her a cup of coffee and she waited even longer as he began dropping ingredients into the bowl. He was making sad bread, but he was making it with love. When the villagers gathered to taste the complicated flavors of his broken heart, that love intensified and for the first time in a long time, Philip was whole again.

Every day after that Pokie began to meet him at the bakery either before or after her route depending on when the gifts appeared. Sometimes accompanied by her dad other times by herself. Seeing her reminded Philip that even though kindness or time alone could not heal a broken heart together they worked miracles.

As for the haunting memories of Mr. Morris. They never left Philip but with time he could summon them up and draw a laugh or a smile when he needed one. Philip ran that bakery with a strange combination of pride and sadness and he always remembered to bring Henesy home a Dad Sandwich every single night.

Chapter 8

Darkness

Three more years went by. Pokie still visited Philip every morning. They often sat together, drinking the first cups of coffee from the kettle, and playing what always turned out to be a brief game of chess. Poecilatheria with her nexus keeper's gift for understanding how things worked, could always see around any gambit that Philip tried. Even when he stayed up the night before reading about chess, she was fast to change the position of her pieces and end the game. This was fine because there was work for both of them to be doing.

When she wasn't delivering gifts, she was delivering herself, talking to people when they were lonely, worried, or sad. They always seemed to seek her out. She didn't offer any solutions for the problems that vexed them. She just listened but in a deep way. The way that she sat with him after Mr. Morris passed. She couldn't solve any of their problems but just by being available, she offered up some small needed measure of comfort and the world around her grew a little less sad.

Philip warned her about the thin walls but people often found her in the bakery and so, without meaning to, he often heard secrets that were not meant for his ears. For his part, because he didn't want to hurt his friend or anyone else, those secrets died with him.

Sometimes, Poecilatheria came early to watch him bake. There was a range of expressions conveying a depth of emotions as he kneaded the bread, smelled the ingredients in search of just the right spice and talked to the fire but it was love and joy she watched for. Seeing him consumed by his art was infectious and consuming.

It was only three years but they were both very young so it may as well have been a lifetime. Something was changing. She used to feel so comfortable and safe around him. She still felt safe but something made her heart pound like she was in danger. She forgot her words. She almost lost a chess game once. She dropped everything. She imagined that a look on his face or the flavor of his new creations was his way of telling her that he loved her. Just as she tried in a million small ways to tell him that she was also in love with him. Something changed. It changed so much that other people were beginning to notice.

When her dad was well enough to accompany her, he always asked to stop at the bakery. When they got there he would just ask for a coffee and push himself into a corner, hiding behind the covers of a book with a stupid sly smile pasted on his face.

The king couldn't help but comment on how incredibly clumsy Pokie and Philip got when they were together. She spilled glasses of water and apologized profusely. Philip dropped the dough and cursed his hands. He had never dropped dough in the past. Their eyes locked and they giggled. Sam and

Henesy, if they were together, often shared secret smiles that caused both Pokie and Philip to blush.

In his head, the king imagined them walking down the aisle tripping over each other's feet while joking, oblivious to anyone else in the room. He imagined that royal decree would be fine with this sort of arrangement because she was sort of a princess in her own right, heiress of the doublewide next to the Nexus.

All of these dreams came crashing down around the king on the night he awoke, cold with sweat, he could swear he heard her scream. He charged from his room, throwing his boots on and alerting the guard. Something is wrong.

Philip was waiting for him in the main chamber, his eyes filled with tears. "Did you feel it too dad?"

"Yes, something's wrong. Something's very wrong,"the king answered.

"The Nexus," Philip said. "I can feel the sadness."

Even before they were close enough to hear it with their ears, they heard it with their hearts. Pokie was screaming in the yard.

"No, no, no, no, Daddy! No, no, not like this!" The Nexus itself was growing and shrinking, flashing violently blue then red and the words she screamed cascaded from somewhere inside. "No, no, no, no, you can't die daddy! You can't die!"

She ran to the carriage begging for help. Nothing could be done. Sam lay on the ground, his face twisted, his hand clutching his chest. "I don't know what happened. I don't know. He can't die, he can't die… I can't carry him. Help me get him to the Nexus. Help me get him to mom. Maybe she can help him, maybe she can!" Her voice was broken, frantic.

"I will help you move him but I need you to know this now." Henesy said. He could feel the bubble rising through his chest. "She can't help him. She won't. He's gone."

"I don't understand, she loves him. I know it, she really loves him."

"I know she does, " the king said. Scooping up the body of someone who was once his sworn enemy for such a stupid reason. "I know she loves him. That is why she won't help. It is his time. If he remains any longer, he won't be himself."

"I don't understand." She buried herself in Philip's arms then and he just held her, wishing there was something, anything he could say to make it better. Having buried Mr. Morris he knew that there wasn't. Death was hell.

"Bring him to me." A soft sweet voice called through the void. The king hoisted the body of his now friend up, his heart being scrambled like pulp in a blender with each passing second. He could feel that old temper raging inside of him. He wanted nothing more than to march through the door and to punch that stupid squid square in the face.

"Save him, please save him!" Pokie begged.

"I'm sorry," the creature answered back. "I'm so sorry."

"What good are you then!" she spat, running from the Nexus into the darkness.

Henesy looked at Philip. "She wants to be alone," He said. Don't let her be alone." Philip nodded and turned to the door following behind as fast as he could.

"You wanted to be alone with me. We are now alone," the creature said.

"I get that I wasn't a good man. I get it. I've learned. I've changed but was I really such a bastard that you would curse me with that book?" His voice was stern and pointed.

"I gave you enough knowledge to make a choice. I gave you many choices and so far you have chosen wisely."

"I can't get it out of my head but of course, you know that. It's like an infection. Why me? Why would you show just me that?"

"Because I know you are terrible and I know you are wonderful. Because you, more than so many others, understand perfectly that nothing is all black or white. That there are so many other colors. You are not a good man king, but you are not a bad man either. You are weak. I know you will fail but I also believe that of everyone I know, you can triumph because you are stronger than you know."

"It's like you're asking me to do that, to live longer than any man ever. To have to bury my boy. My perfect sweet boy. I hid that goddamn book. I threw away all of the keys and I have it guarded against everyone including myself but it won't do a damn bit of good, will it, because those words are magic. I could recite them cover to cover, even after all these years."

"One drop of my blood gives you a thousand years of life," the creature said with unusual coldness.

"And the ability to kill you. Eldritch Kindness. Hmpff, at least the Eldritch Horror is forthright about his cruelty. Sam was a good man. He didn't deserve this!" the king shouted.

"Nobody deserves it, as you may soon know if you so choose."

"Mark my words. You've damned us both, beast!"

The beast jutted a tentacle forward, dangling from a silver thread was a tiny vial containing a shimmering black-blue substance. "Then you have already decided. We shall see if either of us are damned or not. We shall see."

Henesy yanked the vile from the thread with an angry jerk. "Even after I lost my wife, I still found a way to love you but I hate you now. I really hate you!" With a flick, the drop poured from the vile into his mouth. He winced, gagged, and stormed from Nexus. "What have I done?" he thought. "My god, what have I done?"

"Do try to be good." The monster spoke inside of his head.

"For Philip," Henesy answered. "Not for you." He saw a spider scurrying on the ground and threw his foot upon it. It crunched into an unrecognizable goo with spider-like legs. Everything he read was true. The beast held no power over him anymore. He could kill if he wanted and none of its protections would stop him. "Not for you." He repeated.

In the distance, he saw the shadows of Philip and Pocelatheria. She was sobbing uncontrollably into his arms. "For Philip," he repeated once more, before joining them in grief.

CHAPTER 9

JUST HERE

There is something far worse than seeing someone you care about die. That is seeing somebody that you care for stop living and still survive. This is what Philip saw happen to Poecilatheria the very second her father passed. He wasn't sure he would ever get to see the infectious awkward joy she filled every room with ever again.

She still delivered the gifts, this was her duty. It was at the very least what she had promised her father she would do when he was gone but Pocelatheria no longer cared to see them or to talk with the lonely. Instead, she woke up before morning when the rest of the village slumbered and left those gifts on their doorsteps. It was easier that way, more efficient and she didn't have to hear the constant stream of reminders echoing her grief. Every time she was caught it was the same thing. "I'm so sorry. Your father was a good man," as if she needed a perfect stranger to tell her that.

She didn't go to the bakery anymore either. Reminders of Sam were everywhere in that place and even the smell of the bread brought her to her knees. It didn't stop her from lingering across the street well before it opened and peering in the window hoping to catch a glimpse of a shadow and then there was that. She felt the spark, she knew that there had been something starting between her and Philip but the longer she stayed away, the harder it was to face him until finally she was convinced that he would never be able to forgive her for staying away for so long. She couldn't help but think her life before had been good, too good, which was why everything seemed so awful now.

Sometimes from the other side of that darkened window, Philip watched back. He wished now that he had learned to be a man of words as opposed to a man of bread. He knew that every time she smelled it, she felt the ghost of Sam. When he lost Morris he leaned into those reminders but he could see her leaning away. What the hell could he do to fight that? Say, "sorry about your dad, he was a good man, here have a dad sandwich?" No, there was nothing.

One day there was almost something, a glimpse from the past when he happened to come late to the bakery to find her paused on her route. Upon first glimpse of a human shadow, she belted out. "Don't say it. I don't want to hear sorry about your dad or that he was a good man."

"I won't. I'm just here..."

"Here if you need anything? Please, not that either..."

"No. I'm just here, now. I miss you Pokie." She smiled a little sorry but he knew if he fell into those eyes he would drown in their sorrow.

"Mind if I sit with you?" he asked.

"Actually, she answered. "I'd like that." So they sat together for about an hour, waiting on the sun but not saying anything. Still, somehow their silence spoke volumes and though it didn't fix anything, it brought them both some measure of comfort. He didn't dare tell her that the only reason he was running late was that the door to his chamber was covered in spider webs and didn't open until the exact moment it needed to, for him to catch her there. She still kept the agreements but she wasn't on speaking terms with her mom right then.

Have you ever noticed how two different people can hear the same thing and receive two different messages? This was how it was when Philip's door webbed over. It stopped him from leaving early so he could watch Poecilatheria from the window and helped him find the courage to talk to her again. Had he been paying attention he would have discovered it was not just his door that was webbed over, but the entire castle. In fact, almost every door, almost every window. Had he looked up he would have seen tables, chairs, large decorative suits of armor, and swords hanging from threads that were hundreds of feet off of the ground. All manned by a plague of spiders that undulated in every shadow. He didn't notice so many things, so while the message he got seemed tender, the message Henesy got was anything but.

"Sir," he was greeted by a guard hanging five feet off of the ground. "We tried. We really did but…"

The king burst into laughter. To anyone present, that laugh was somehow worse than the plague of spiders which had glued everything in the castle (including the guards) into immovable unusable things.

"I've got your message, monster." He called out. "Please, don't torment these men. They haven't done anything. I have."

With those words, the shadows seemed to barf forward. It was a billowing cloud of spiders consuming every inch of every wall, all of the webs, and all of the people. The titter-tatter of their billions of legs became a deafening roar that lasted for a full ten seconds. They covered the king's face and he could feel them writhing beneath his pant legs and under his shirt. Compared to those ten seconds of sheer repulsion and dread, the next thousand years would seem quick. While he was covered in spiders, knowing full well that it was a punishment for killing one and that the only choice he had was to endure it, those ten seconds passed slower than a snail crossing a salt flat.

And then, it was done. Guards, tables, and chairs all lay strewn across the floor. Nothing was damaged but it all looked disordered, dirty with webs, and ill at ease.

"What was that?" one of the guards cried.

"A reminder. " Henesy answered him. "A reminder that I don't have to be a monster." His boots were the last thing to drop. They fell on his head. When he picked them up he could still see the greasy smear on the right boot where a spider not much different from the swarm in his house, met its fate.

CHAPTER 10

THE GIFT

Poecilatheria had sat with Philip for longer than she intended to. There was no way she was going to beat the sun back home today and yet somehow, she was okay with that. They hadn't said anything. exchanged any awkward glances or started tripping over themselves. They just sat together in darkness and silence. That was enough. Somehow Philip just being there then, sitting in darkness and silence with her. It made the whole world seem to sting a little less.

The last gift she had to deliver that day was a baby blanket, something was weird about this one though. Just like her dad, when it came to the gifts, she always seemed to know where they should go and how to make them work. It was a blanket, so she didn't expect any explanation for that. But where did it belong? At first, she thought she knew but it felt somehow wrong.

She knew that Mr. Henderson's widow was expecting a baby. Nobody else in the village was. Pokie set the blanket on the porch and turned to go but she just knew somehow that the gift hadn't been delivered. Her feet would not lift, not in that direction. Then she heard it, the unmistakable high shrill shriek of a tiny human. "Not Carrol, not her too." It felt wrong because the blanket was never intended to be the gift.

Pokie's knocks were met by tiny desperate screams. So she turned the latch. It didn't turn, not at first but then one at a time from behind the door, she could hear bolts shifting, metal clanking, and pins moving and the door seemed to open by itself. A thin thread of silk betrayed the identity of the secret locksmith.

Carrol was dead on the floor. Between her legs, a pool of blood, and a baby that his birth mom had never even gotten the chance to hold.

"Come here, little fellow. I want you to meet your birth mom." Pokie wrapped the child in a blanket and propped up the corpse of his mother so that she could support the hand and nestle the baby in them. "She would have been a great mom, you would have turned up a good man, I know it. Life has made different plans for us though. Somehow it seems I was meant to be a gift to you. You are in need of a new family. I don't know if I can do a good enough job or not but I'll try. Guess this means I have to go makeup with your grandma huh? She's a little crazy but I know she's mostly good."

Chapter 11

You're an Idiot, Philip.

She stopped in the bakery to tell Philip about her last delivery. This time it was more to see him in an official capacity as the prince than to visit. The guards would soon be in for their morning coffee and he could send them to Catrol's hut to make sure her body found its way into the ground. It was best to take care of these things as fast as possible. The prohibition on violence may have stopped people from dying of murder but it did nothing to stop bloating, flies, rats, and diseases.

"Will he, um, need a father?" Philip tried to ask but Pokie's glare warned him that he had stumbled somewhere no man ever wanted to be.

"Philip, I love you but you're an idiot." Pokie snorted.

"Wait…love? You said you love me!"

"I said you're an idiot!" the bakery door slammed shut behind her. Later, when he retold the story to the king he said the same thing as Pokie but in a more compassionate voice.

"You're an idiot son. I know you two love each other. Sam knew it. Hell, rocks that are completely incapable of thinking know how you two feel about one another. She doesn't want you to ease her parenting burdens. Well, eventually she will because little babies can be nightmares but that's not what she wants. She doesn't want a business proposition. Swoon her you damn fool!"

"Dad, I don't know if I can swoon."

"I may not know much but here's one thing I know. Everyone has a way of showing love that only they can show. You need to find yours, but there is something you also need to know Philip. You can't expect her to marry you and move into the castle with us. No matter how much she loves you, her life is tied to the Nexus. Her family will be tied to the Nexus for at least a thousand years. That being said, should you discover how to swoon, the castle is mainly here to protect the crown from people who might murder us. I don't see that as much of an issue anymore. Do you understand?."

"Yes," Philip answered.

"Good. Because I want grandbabies damn it, lots of them. A whole army of princes and princesses. Now go get her, you idiot!"

After receiving the advice, Philip left, not stopping to ask about the cleaning crews who were scraping soot from the castle walls or why everything smelled like smoke. Everyone was talking about the fire at the castle that Henesy started by trying to clean up after a swarm of spiders. Much to Henesys relief, Philip's mind was too distracted by Poecilotheria that day, to hear a single word of it.

"Atroxrobustus," as the beast had dubbed the baby, had not quit screaming since she brought him home. Pokie was in a state that went beyond tiredness or exhaustion. Her thoughts felt like thick viscous rubber things that she could barely see to wade through. The tiniest moment of respite had been granted to her until some idiot knocked on her door and Atroxrobustus began producing a noise that split Pokie's brain in half as it echoed out of the back of her skull.

She could feel her hair standing up on end. Her clothes, the same ones she was wearing when she found grandma's little demon, were stained with various bodily fluids and there was Philip standing on the other side of the door holding a cloth sack and staring back at her like he had lost every drop of sense in his body.

"It's really not a good time Philip. I haven't slept at all. I may never sleep again and I know, I just know that mother is highly amused by this."

"I just made a new sandwich today and I wanted you to test it. I'm thinking of calling it the, *You're right I'm a total idiot and I love you too but was just too much of a coward to say it, on molasses-wry sandwich* I know the title is a work in progress but…" He paused for the longest time and so did Atrox. "Look, I know that you are tied to the Nexus and that you could never marry me and move to the castle and all of that but I don't care. I just know that my life is better with you in it. I will take that in any way I can. I'm in love with you. I have loved you since…"

He looked up to see there was nothing on her face. She said nothing and didn't move. She gave no feedback or response whatsoever.

"Oh god, no I, I messed everything up didn't I?." Philip stammered as Pocilatheria just stood there in disbelief staring back. "Please don't hate me. Please don't." The sandwich in the sack fell from his hands and he pivoted away quickly trying to hide the tiny dots of tears getting ready to come pouring out of his eyes.

Pokie rested the baby in the crib and darted after him calling out, 'Wait, DAMMIT wait!. I couldn't tell you how I feel because…"

She quit using words after that. When she kissed him the whole kingdom was awash in violent blue light as the Nexus shined with approval.

The guards in the castle were at first terrified and then confused when their king blurted out, "Damn boy, and you said you don't know how to swoon!" The next morning Pokie and Philip shared that sandwich. It was delicious.

Chapter 12

Everyone Dies.

A lot of things change over the next seventeen years. Prince Philip now resides full-time with his wife at the doublewide. She drives him to the bakery every morning before delivering the gifts in person by day. Atrox goes from an apprehensive baby to a spirited child and into a teenager living two lives. One life in the Nexus distributing gifts with his mom and one life in the courtyards of his grandfather's castle.

The whole village is gifted digital cameras which they use to record their lives onto albums. The king, after a long spell, quits offering unsolicited advice to his son about how to go about making babies. Even the trees in the village change. Shrubs that were planted to help block the light from the Nexus, which seemed to be getting brighter and bigger with every passing day, now tower.

The one thing that doesn't change; however, is the appearance of Henesy's age. While the rest of the world was getting older, the king seemed to be paused within a moment. Philip, who now looked more like Henesy's brother than his son, brought it up several times but soon learned not to press the issue. Henesy for his part told Philip, "There is something we need to talk about, when I'm ready." He never seemed ready to talk about it though.

If he was being honest with himself Philip wasn't ready either. He was relieved for more reasons than one that his dad had found some sort of fountain of youth. He would have been happy for him but he could tell that the King wasn't happy. There was something about his seeming immortality that terrified the king. Philip wasn't ready to find out what that was. He just wanted to keep his dad and he wanted to keep his life with his wife next to the Nexus. Whatever it was, Philip knew it would spoil those things.

To Philip, the way things were, was good. It wasn't always easy but it was good. There were occasional fights and setbacks in the process of joining their lives together. Maintaining love takes work but Philip was always willing to do that work. So in spite of any little spats between them, he woke up feeling more in love with Pokie every day.

If things hadn't been so good, they wouldn't have felt so bad. It is the sad truth that anyone who shares a good life with another person soon has to face. So it was that one day, Philip woke up when the sun was already bright in the sky and placed his hands on his wife's shoulder saying "Hunny, wake up we're late." and found her body cold.

Just as he realized what had occurred, so did the Nexus. Their bonding had once turned the day into night. Their parting turned the day into night for three whole days. Afterward, the first gifts Atrox had to deliver by himself were journals with very specific requests printed on top of them. "Record what you know to be true about the Nexus and The Kindness. Keep these truths in your families."

The journals came with a premonition. It was the darkest thing he had ever conceived in his life. He was not to tell his father or his grandfather anything. If he did, the keepers of truth would die.

That morning he confronted Grandma. "They're not bad people," he shouted as he crossed into the Nexus.

The monster lowered herself, showing no offense. She knew this conversation was coming after all. "No, they are not. Your father is a beautiful soul. Your grandfather is…complicated. Neither of them would seek to harm any of the villagers, but your father keeps no secrets from the king and the king has taken it upon himself to face all of the darkness in our world alone. He made a choice to do this because whether he chose it or not, someone would have to. Many men would go into this choice seeking power and that power would consume them but Henesy knew just what it would cost and how much it would hurt.

He thinks he has failed but that man has a love in his heart that not even he can understand yet he will be tested and he will be corrupted, if only for a while. I gave you a strong name child because the task at hand is going to be hard. You must love the king and teach your children to love him, even after he gets hard to love. You must face darkness and stay kind. If you do this many will think you are weak but it is the definition of real strength."

Her words sunk into his heart in much the same way the words of the book had tattooed themself to the king's brain.

Three days later Atrox and Philip were awoken by a loud growling noise to see two yellow lights shining through the window. Something slammed at the door, "Dad?"

Philip sat up. "I guess we need to answer."

The man at the door was dressed in the strangest garb Atrox had ever seen. He had a blue single-piece uniform and atop his head, a hat with a duck-like bill marked with the words *Delivery Max*.

"Listen, kid, someone paid a lot of money to get this to you. I don't even know how I found this place but I would like to know just what the hell I'm delivering? The box keeps moving. Is this some sort of animal?" He looked at the box in his hands. "You're Atrox Robustus, right? Here," he passed the box forward. "I will need a signature of course and then maybe you could tell me how to get back to Madison?"

"Madison?" Atrox Robustus was confused.

"Yeah. Madison, Wisconsin. Where else? But sign first." He handed Atrox a small box and looked as if he was expecting something, he then motioned to the pen dangling from the box. Atrox had never seen such a device but reasoned that he could pick up the weird pen attached to the cord and write his name on the surface of the box. When he was done he handed it back to the courier who went to his truck and pulled out a bigger box. Giant red letters on the outside of the box read, "*EXTREMELY FRAGILE AND DANGEROUS, DO NOT DROP, KICK OR SHAKE THIS BOX.*"

"Ok now, two things. After the address line. I got here by directions that said to follow the glowing mushrooms. I mean, I found you but what the hell, and second what's in the box? I mean, a million-dollar tip? Don't worry I'm not going to rat you out but it's drugs, isn't it? Or some kind of exotic animal, or maybe an exotic animal stuffed with drugs, I have to know."

Still confused, Atrox pulled open the seal and the driver looked inside and screamed. "Oh no, I don't do human trafficking. I lied. I'm calling the po..." There was a sudden flash of light. Both the courier and the square metal monster behind him disappeared.

Atrox reached down and pulled the tiny human out of the packing peanuts and bubble wrap. It giggled. Atrox gasped and stared at his father. "I'm not ready for this dad."

Philip giggled. "No one ever is. Especially you Nexus keepers. Let me see my grandson."

The monster named him Hapalochlaena.

The years raced on and the baby grew into a tall broad chested, bright-eyed, bearded man. Much like the case of Poecilatheria and Sam, Atrox fell dead just as his son was old enough to take over the family business.

While having a grandchild was a short respite from the pain of losing his wife, Philip was lost when his only child, who he hoped would one day bury him, was placed into the arms of his grandmother, never to be seen again.

.

One-day Hapalochlaena fell asleep and woke up to find a baby in his arms. The day that happened, Philip, who was never a man of religion, started to pray to anyone who would listen. He prayed that death would take him in the next fifteen years. His prayers were unanswered and one day when he was well into his nineties, Hapalochlaena died.

Scolopendrasubsnipes was already trained and making deliveries soon to be a mother herself.

Through it all King Henesy looked the same, almost.

Losing so many non-heir heirs after opening his heart to them, had put new lines in the corners of his eyes. His son was nearing a hundred and years seemed to be passing like months. The damn kid still made him sandwiches every day. He needed a cane to walk and yet he was still going to the bakery, toiling over a hot stove to feed the village before returning to the castle where he would sit with his dad and wait without saying a word. In part enjoying the company and in part waiting for answers about why it was the king never aged and why that topic seemed to worry the king so much.

"You were but a child" the king one day began, "Strike that. Before you were born, I was not the man you know today. The whole damned village was falling around me. The rift existed but nobody knew about the creature inside of it. There were whispers of a monster, something called an Eldritch Terror that would drive men mad if they even happened to glance upon it. There wasn't enough food to go around, and most of the mushrooms that grew here were poisonous. Our kingdom was a hellscape and nothing I did seemed to make it any better."

"With so many people struggling to find food half the town was made of thieves. They weren't bad people, they were just desperate to survive. I had grown up with too much of everything. Too much money, too much food, too much power. Even as the world around me was dying from starvation, I was getting fat. The worst part was the one way I could think to control the thieving was to kill everyone who was caught stealing. I killed a lot of men, son. I wish I hadn't but I didn't know of any other way.

There was one thief in particular who was so brazen and so lucky. I wanted to kill him more than any of the others. Thing is, he was also braver than any of my men and he had a kind heart. Half the time the guards let him slide and the other half he would charge headfirst into the craziest places and none of the guards dared to follow. That's how Sam discovered the Nexus and the monster inside. It was not an Eldritch terror but an Eldritch Kindness, the other side of that coin. It is a beast of indefinable love and hope, drawn to our desperation, and drawn to me. For as terrible as I was, I had one redeeming quality. The woman I loved, I loved with every ounce of my soul. Back then that was about the only good thing about me."

"It was Sam who made the simplest gesture of goodwill and love that allowed this beast to come into our world. It wasn't just here to make things all sunshine and roses though. It was here to test us and the test isn't over. When it took away the worst of our desperation the people of this village rose to the challenge. They quit stealing from one another. They quit causing useless drama and we made our own little heaven."

"By coming into our world it curses itself though, real good can't exist in a vacuum without evil. There is no love without the potential for hate. Understand that this was not a choice that was easy. After your mom passed I

72

became obsessed with stopping death. I knew that somehow that creature that had given us so many other great things would be the key to nobody ever having to endure the pain of burying their loved ones again. But that is not why…"

Henesy paused and sighed, staring out the window for several seconds before regaining his composure. "None of the books from our world seemed to offer any answers. I might have even given up if not for one of the gifts. It was a book sealed in parchment that told me exactly how I could end death but what it also told me…"

"I don't know how to say this next part," the king sighed again. "Because when it came into our world, it cursed itself. It had no choice but to surrender a single drop of its blood and had it not been me, it may have been anyone. This drop gave me one thousand years of life and all of the suffering that went along with it. I knew that if I accepted this drop it could corrupt me. At some point, it has to because love cannot survive without the potential for hate. I am the only person in this village with the ability to kill another. I crushed a spider once just to see if it was real. I don't want to test that in the future. That is my test though. One day, you will die and I will have to find a way to keep my heart intact. If I start to slip into the darkness, it will be harder for me than it will be for any other man to pull myself out, because I accepted the curse.

There are only three outcomes. Two of which I can live with. When my thousand years are over, if I succeed, I may take the place of the Kindness. Or if I can learn to let go, I may be given a passage to Judith. The third option, what is fated to happen if I cannot keep love in my heart, is that I may be cursed to become an Eldritch Terror. I will destroy not just this world but the whole damn universe, and so many others.'

'

"Dad…" Philip sighed looking deep into Henesys watery eyes.

"Just tell me, son, in spite of all the pain, in spite of the loss. Has it all been worth it? Have you had a good life." The king was crying half afraid of what Philip was about to say.

"Yes, dad. I have known sadness but I have known love. True love, ten times more than any man deserves. I wouldn't trade a second of it. Not one second with Pokie or Atrox, my grandbabies or Mr. Morris, and least of all with you."

"Then there is hope," the king cried.

He could see by the look in Henesys eyes just why the king had waited until this day to tell him. The king knew something and now he did too.

"I love you, dad. I'm going to miss you when I'm gone." By the way of last words Philip decided that those were pretty damn good ones. He closed his eyes and let all of the burdens and constraints of the world fall off of him.

"Monster," the king's voice echoed through the Nexus. Monster, I can't do this. Give him back to me, do you hear? Give him back. Take my life. I don't want it anymore. Just give him a drop too. Something, anything but don't make me do this, I can feel myself failing."

"Everyone fails for a time," the monster answered. It lowered its terrible face to meet the king's square on. I know you will fail but you are strong, you are beautiful. You have a way of coming back."

"I thought that once too but I know it's a lie. A stupid lie that I told myself to justify a selfish impulse. My baby." The king clutched the body of his son just as he had clutched the body of his wife a century ago. "Please, I don't deserve this. He didn't deserve this. Sam, Pokie, Atrox, and…" a tentacle reached through the darkness seizing the boy. "Their lives were all too short. A hundred years and it passed in a blink!"

"Their lives were exactly the lengths that their lives were going to be. That is not my work. Everyone dies my king, everyone except for maybe you."

"I won't let it happen. I won't let myself become that thing and kill all of those people. I'll see to it!"

"That is why, I wanted it to be you, king," the monster retorted.

"There is another way you know. I could kill you. I could cut you up and turn you into monster sandwiches and feed it to everyone so that when I turn there won't be a damn soul left that I can harm! If I can't feed myself then I won't have the power to jump into other worlds!"

"I see," said the monster. "You have nine hundred years to think about this. If you really think that is what's best then there isn't much I can do to stop you, is there?. Either way, there will be an Eldritch, either of love and hope or one of insanity and murder. Don't lose sight king. Find your way back to me. Find your way back to your heart."

CHAPTER 13

A BAD PLAN

Scolopendrasubsnipes was in her 90s when she passed. She raised a
son and watched her granddaughter learn and take over the family business.
King Henesy may have rejoiced that one of his grandchildren got to live a full
life but at some point in her early twenties they started seeing each other less
and less until one day when she arrived at the castle gates to bring him
presents wrapped in parchment with the word *grandaddy* scrawled across the
top and enclosed in hearts, she discovered that the gates had been locked and
so was his heart.

That was the last time in a long time that any of the nexus keepers
were able to talk to the king. He didn't have the heart to lose any more family
and had convinced himself that the best way to protect himself from that was
to never meet them in the first place.

He still looked towards the Nexus every day, remembering how it lit
up the sky when his son worked up the courage to speak what was in his

heart. He would dream about them at night in spite of himself but he would not, could not, let them back into his heart. Over the years the gifts piled up, leaving his great-granddaughter to wonder how it was that she had hurt him so badly. When she died an old woman, she took that pain with her to her grave in the monster's heart and the Nexus seemed to fade by degrees. So, in turn, did Henesy's heart.

Upon her death, he had flyers pinned up explaining that the beast was not a Kindness but a Terror. He knew he could not order the town folks to refuse the gifts but he cautioned against accepting them. Spinning a tale about how the nexus keepers were unwitting slaves to the monster's evil game. By accepting the gifts, the king explained, you were hurting these poor orphans who were stolen from their murdered parents. Nobody believed it, not at first but those messages were not meant to impact the current generation. He had learned this from his time in politics, before the onset of the Kindness. A lie repeated often enough begins to sound more like the truth than the truth itself.

Soon after he passed a law to stop people from sharing what he called *fake news* about the monster. Anyone caught referring to it as a Kindness or praising it for its generosity would be sentenced to a month in the dungeon and as the days turned into years, which turned into centuries, the Nexus got dimmer and dimmer.

Villagers started returning the gifts, often the very thing they needed to make their lives better, for fear that they were torturing the Gatekeeper. The gatekeepers themselves started keeping some of the gifts, they knew who wouldn't appreciate what they had to offer after all. Besides, some of the things the creature gifted were better than the receiver deserved. There was still kindness in their hearts but it was twisted or tainted by their perception of how other people thought of them. The villagers thought they were weird, stupid slaves.

It took centuries but the light darkened the doorway and the beast inside began to starve and weaken. King Henesy was hoping this would happen. The disrespect for the nexus keepers twisted into contempt and while Henesy hated to see his heirs tormented so, it was the one way that he knew would weaken the beast enough for him to kill it with a single blow.

He didn't believe the lies he was spreading. He didn't hate the beast. He even regretted every step he took but he began to believe that he would do anything possible, if he could make death die.

He was twisting inside, he could feel the inevitability of his transition. If nothing else, he would do one last good thing while there was still good inside of him to do it. When his years ran out and the choice was made, King Henesy aimed to destroy that beast and himself too. When he was done his entire kingdom would be granted a gift that the monster, with all its magic, would never give them. They would live forever. This brings us back to the beginning. near the ending of this story.

Chapter 14

Breaking The Nexus

Earwigregalusis's father, Macrothele, never could bring the Nexus back to the way it was described, though he and his ancestors tried. It had been harder and harder to get anyone to accept any gifts in the past hundred years. When they pulled their cart through town, most of the adults glowered or looked away trying not to notice them. The kindest of the intended receivers would say, "No thank you." Those who were not so kind cursed, spat, or threw rocks that never came close.

Every day they received the gifts and tried to deliver them and every day they were attacked. When Earwig asked why they tried so hard his dad always had the same response.

"Sometimes you have to choose between what's right and what's easy. When that happens, choose what's right."

Every day was a bad day, but the day it happened was one of the worst bad days Earwig could remember ever having. The king's flyers were everywhere. Anytime the slightest breeze made one flap Earwigregalusis winced in almost physical pain.

"It's not right. He's lying, why do we just let him lie like that?" Earwigregalusis protested.

Macrothele just smiled a soft comforting smile. "I know what you're feeling, son," he sighed. "There's nothing that can be done for it. Part of this is my fault. I haven't brought you into the Nexus with me. I should have, long ago. You need to see your grandma to understand."

"That thing is not my grandmother. She is a monster. A monster we serve by bringing trinkets to unappreciative idiots who don't deserve the goat crap on the road!"

"Now you listen to me boy and listen well. You shouldn't talk about her like that. Everything she has done has been to try and heal this broken world." Macrothele was not a person who raised his voice ever but this time his voice boomed, his fists shook and his face turned dark red.

Earwig snorted. "Yeah, fat bit of good that's done. Everyone hates us. They hate you. They hate me!"

"They don't hate us. They just.... don't understand. It's not their fault. They can't understand. Not with these damn flyers being pinned up every day."

As they neared the Nexus, the thousands of posters, naming wanted heretics and decrying the gatekeepers as dangerous criminals thinned out until the only ones that could be seen were those that had been stripped from their posts by the wind. No one came here anymore. That made it more comfortable but the comfort was slight. No one coming near the Nexus also hurt.

They were home, in their yard, which looked like a garbage dump where rejected gifts rusted into broken useless husks. It was hard to understand. There was once a time when people had electricity, plumbing and all of these things enriched them but now it wasn't worth it.

Beyond the protection of the Nexus, the king seized any gifts he found out were accepted. Not that they weren't dropping enough garbage off outside of the castle gates. What the kingdom was in desperate need of was a landfill that wasn't their yard. Between the rejected gifts and the flyers you could swim through the garbage.

There was a new sort of mushroom growing in the yard. It was huge and red. It looked like an apple and smelled savory and meaty. It was like nothing he had ever smelled before. Macrothele seized it on sight, giving it a sniff. Just because all of the mushrooms were safe didn't make them tasty.

"Want one, " he asked his son, sinking his teeth deep into the meat. And then it happened…

Sometime in the last few centuries, people forgot that the promise of every mushroom in the kingdom being edible was only for a thousand years.

No sooner had he swallowed the red mushroom bite, than he fell to the ground writhing and twitching.

The Nexus darkened even more.

Macrothele's voice was weak and strained. "Go get Nancy. Don't let the guards see you!"

Nancy was an old woman who lived in the last little bunch of houses before the Nexus dead zone. A week ago, she had accepted a book about medicine and even went as far as to whisper, "thank you," before disappearing behind a closed door and blacked out windows.

Earwigregalius's heart was in his hand as he threw one foot in front of the other, as fast as his legs would move him, back toward town. He was trying to be cautious but in his desperate attempt to find help, it was hard to notice anything. Not until he charged into a group of kids fruitlessly stomping on top of a spider. They couldn't harm it. It wasn't one of the venomous ones, so it couldn't harm them either but it tried. The poor beast was striking again and again, wearing itself out as the boy's feet danced all around it.

"Hey look it's Bug Boy! What's your name again, Ear Mite?" They lost interest in the spider and started kicking and punching at him. None of their blows struck but he winced all the same and as he did they laughed. "I wish I could hit you, you freak! I'd splatter your brains all over the ground. Ear Mite, Ear Mite!"

Earwigregalus stood angry, squaring off with his adversaries. He took a wild swing and something happened that hadn't happened in a thousand years. His knuckles struck bone and the bully dropped to the ground screaming and crying. He crawled backward, leaping to his feet as the whole group darted away. Once they felt like they had reached a safe distance they stared back in surprise and terror.

There was blood on the nexus keeper's hands that wasn't his. There was a thought in his head that didn't belong there either. He didn't just want to hurt that kid. He wanted to kill him but it didn't matter really, the only thing that mattered was getting Nancy. The only thing that mattered was saving his dad.

She was outside running towards him. She clutched her illegal book tight in her hands for all the world to see in broad daylight. as if she was challenging them to take it.

"My dad, my dad," Earwig cried. Nancy's dark arms fell around him.

"I know, I know," she whispered. "She told me this would happen." He caught the look in her eyes and immediately understood. Unlike him, Nancy actually knew his grandma.

"I messed up. I hurt somebody. They're going to come for me aren't they?"

"Probably." Nancy answered. "Violence is back. Things are going to get bad.".

He bothered her with his worries, all the way back to the house, but Nancy didn't betray any signs of annoyance. Her answers were short but sweetly intended and her voice kind. It seemed as though she was the last person in the world without darkness in her heart. Even Earwig himself, a nexus keeper who was supposed to be some sort of infinitely kind beacon of light, found his mind intruded upon by fantasies of murder.

"What do I do now?" he asked. In the distance, two guards approached. He had never seen them anywhere near the Nexus before. They always avoided it. They avoided him and his dad also but something had changed. Both of the guards appeared to be big men but one of them was almost seven feet tall.

Nancy stooped by Macrothe. "Nancy," his broken voice whispered. "I'm here Macro, I'm here. You just rest. Things are going to work out. You'll see."

"Earwigregalusis Yohonamonstavitchnic! Macrothele Yohonamonstavitchnic! Nancy Williams! By order of the king, you are all under arrest!" One of the guard's voices boomed.

Nancy looked at Earwigregalusis. Her eyes flashed with purpose and desperation. "It's time you learned the truth. Go to your grandmother."

"No," Earwigregalusis screamed. "She's not my Grandma. I hate that monster. I hate this Nexus and this job and I hate that stupid name. I have never in my life ever felt like Earwigregalisus."

The world went black as if whatever was in the Nexus had sucked up the last little bit of light and they would never see the sun again. "You need to go now. You need to know the truth, now!" Nancy shouted. Your dad's life depends on it!"

The options made his stomach churn but Earwig turned and pushed his way into the shrinking Nexus. Once inside, the sun did return but it was dimmer than it had been before. Nancy watched him go and then stood, glaring back at the guards with her hand over her heart and her fingers splayed apart.

You understand that these will work now, right?" the smaller guard asked, drawing his sword.

Nancy nodded, "Yes."

"Then you'll have to forgive me because I don't have the luxury of time." He swung his sword, not at Nancy but at the giant guard beside him, who fell to the ground bleeding and clutching his chest.

"Why?!" the injured guard screamed.

"I am a keeper of truth, and so is she. I do not wish to hurt you any more than I already have but know this. I will not let you leave here until Macrothe is back on his feet."

The injured guard continued to bellow though the wound was mostly superficial. He glared at his friend Jack, who now loomed over him, sword in hand and threatening his life. Jack reached his free hand into his back pocket, pulling out a worn and tired book. He tossed it towards his companion, who opened it, cautiously looking back at his once friend.

He started on the very first page where the instructions said, "write what you know to be true about the monster. There is a big lie that spans the centuries. Our families have been keeping the memories and pictures from a better time. We have recorded how the lie grew and changed over time so that one day the truth may be known by all." The guard looked up at him again.

Right now, you need to see this," Jack continued. "You need to know that I am not betraying you. I am trying to save you and everyone else. So damn it, Leroy, figure this out because I don't want to kill my friend. Nancy will put you right."

We have now arrived back to the point where our story began. After leaving his father on faith, (not in the monster but faith in Nancy) Earwig had spoken to his grandmother and now found himself following a thread as he had been instructed and crossing a sheet of glowing blue webbing that seemed to roll on for infinity. As he traveled, Grandmother's kind voice returned at seemingly random moments but the truth in it seemed to sting and find all of the wounds that had brought him here in the first place.

"I know much of what is going to happen but I don't know everything," Grandmother's voice called as Earwig continued probing the darkness. "I knew that your father would fall ill. I knew that it would bring you here to me because, to me, those things had already happened over a thousand years before now.

I knew when I gave you your sacred name that it wasn't who you were. You are a different sort of Yhonamonstrosavitchnic. You need to seek out your own identity, one that you will come to know yourself. This is not your fault and this is not my fault.

With you, it is not your job to follow a custom that hurts your heart. It is mine to accept you, no matter what you find. Cast aside your guilt child. It won't serve you here. Find your heart."

Blue light emanated from the ground beneath Earwig's feet. It shimmered in the distance and even above him. As he followed the thread, he couldn't help but look down searching for a bearing but there was nothing to look at. Just miles of blue hues which moved as though he was walking upon a massive sheet.

Occasionally, the shadow from some aspect of grandmother pulled his eyes upwards and he would see a bit of a tentacle or spidery leg dip down into his field of view before disappearing in the infinity above. In the tales of the nexus keepers, they described her as bigger than the mountains. He now knew that was because man did not have the words in his vocabulary to describe how big that really was.

Those who had seen her had only ever seen a portion. Her face, a couple of legs, and some tentacles that she brought into their field of view to make them comfortable. People need to be able to have some sort of scope or measure to understand or to feel comfortable. In reality, she could reach up further than any man could see and pull her massive body into that vast oblivion.

His thoughts were brooding. Had she wanted too, she could have grasped him and moved him across this unending plain of tacky sheet-like ground, to some other vista that was closer to wherever it was he needed to be or whatever it was he needed to find.

She did not; however try to shorten his journey and he was too upset to speak to her any more, so he just kept walking. Earwig could feel the hours pass, uncountable and horrifying against the frantic desperation of his father's situation. Outside Macrothele was dying. Outside he was surrounded by enemies in a world that was rediscovering violence. Outside something far more terrible than any nexus monster loomed and there was nothing Earwig could do, except walk. Those hours stacked together, forming what had to be at least a day, then two and then… and then it didn't matter because the thread was leading him into the middle of a vast empty blue glowing void.

More shadows….Something akin to a leg, but shorter and not jointed. It spat out strands of thread or rope. A leg intersected the thread and then everything disappeared above him.

"Where am I?" he called. Not even his voice echoed back. Then he saw it, the source of the shine. A sheet of web wall, each strand glowing faint blue, but amid the millions of strands the light was almost blinding, and where the wall draped around, it arched over a deep black tunnel. The thread led him on.

Chapter 15

The Dark Nexus

The tunnel of webbing grew narrower and narrower until it shrank to a hole barely big enough for Earwigregalus to squeeze through. On the other side, the blackness seemed to radiate. It was glowing inward as though it were made of a darker light. Earwig's hair bristled as he followed the thread now. He was almost entering the black before a tentacle blocked his path.

"It is a dangerous place, where you are going. Before you go farther, you will need to receive three gifts." A glowing blue silken robe fell around his shoulders.

"There is one who looks like me but he is not like me." The threading on the ceiling brightened. It began forming the shape of a hand mirror morphing from blue to green, then to yellow, before it seemed to drip down as a solid object dangling by a thread in front of his face. The reflection in the glass was not him as he was now. Instead, it was him as a child of four, delivering gifts with his father. The townsfolk booed and cursed. They looked aside or glowered in disapproval but the child in the reflection smiled. He was proud of his heritage, proud to be giving people what they didn't know they needed. He could see the secret pain on his father's face. The dueling conflict of Macrothele wanting to shelter his child from the villagers disapproval and the determination to walk him through it with the half-hearted hope that this pain would only make him kinder. He turned the mirror to the beast and saw a hand plucking a spider up from underneath one of his distant ancestors' feet.

"Keep this secret," the monster warned him. "This mirror reflects hidden truth. Not everybody wants to know the truth. You can also use this to find your way back."

The third gift was a picture of his father. "This is the most important item. Remember why you're here. The monster on the other side will try to steal that from you."

The tentacle swirled out of his path revealing the end of the thread and the glowing darkness beyond. Earwig pressed on.

The webs seemed to glow with blackness on this side, radiating shadows like his grandmother's webs had radiated light. This beast, though out of sight, made its presence known immediately with intermittent mocking calls.

"Ahh, a young emissary from my sister's realm? I may not see you but I know exactly where you are. Perhaps sis should have spent less time trying to hide you and more time explaining to you exactly how our webs work." This monster's voice was a masculine tenor with a half-growling rasp to it. Something about the voice told Earwig that he was big, even in terms of mountain-sized monsters.

"Don't worry, young emissary. I won't eat you yet. That would be rude." Shadows moved near him, they danced across the dark webs miles away but the monster didn't reveal himself. The web floor seemed to shift beneath him as the beast rumbled on from the bottom of a funnel that grew at Earwig's feet.

"If I were you, I would go home child. You have no part in this game that has been played over aeons. When the very stars that paint your sky and the universe that holds them were but dreams in the abyss, we were here. Me and my sister, tangled in this web."

A giant beak erupted from beneath him. Two fangs dripped with clear venom on each side and inside of the beak, thousands of smaller toothy mouths attached to eel-like appendages. It was all lunging forward, snapping at Earwig's feet. As it got closer, he could see that between the eel-like mouths, long ivory-curved and black fangs undulated.

Earwig pushed his line of vision outside of the mouth, past the teeth, fangs and tentacles and beyond, to see a monster much like his grandmother; except covered in shimmering gold.

The monster burst forward until all that Earwig could see again was the jagged, squirming, snapping bits beneath the beak. It was about to swallow him. However, the second it seemed that everything sharp and venomous collapsed inward on him, it disappeared and he found he was laying flat, stomach down on the web lining he had been crossing. His hands were buried and stuck inside of the silk, his jaw tight and his eyes half closed.

"Just so you understand, emissary, I could end you anytime I want. But I am curious, so curious. I want to know what will kill you if I don't. What did she tell you, emissary? What web did she spin to lure you off to a land that is sure to kill you? I hope she didn't make you feel important. Know that you don't matter and you might survive."

Earwig said nothing. He tried to stay as still as possible, to breathe as light as he could but try as he might, the thunder of his heart betrayed him.

"She sent you here so you can see and she can know just how I squeezed so much of myself into her world. That is the truth of this young emissary. She can feel me feeding over there, starving her out. There's more darkness than love there these days, isn't there?"

Earwig pulled his hands free from the webs, stood, and began a slow cautious walk. He wished this monster's voice would just fall silent but he knew it wouldn't. Whether it was the truth or lies didn't matter. The monster was attempting to probe his mind, latching on and testing every insecurity it could find. Earwig understood what it was the robe was hiding from it now. It was not his physical body, not his flesh but his thoughts.

"She only cares about your emotions, she doesn't care about you. Her worrying about you would be like you concerning yourself with the life of a flea."

Earwig pressed forward, saying nothing. When his wish did come true and the monster fell silent, it was almost worse. He knew that it was there somewhere, not occupying just one distance but two or three distances on opposite sides of him. He could see its massive shadows just for a second, followed by nothing. Seven times he had to step over human skeletons that seemed to be strewn on the only walkable surface of the web. It looked like they had been there for a long time but he doubted it. It was just the monster probing him, trying to figure out what would make him lose his grip. So Earwig walked on.

Just like it was in grandmother's webs, Earwig walked for what seemed like days. Unlike his time on the other side, he was parched and ravenous for any food he could get his mouth on but there was nothing to be found here.

The walk was beyond excruciating. It seemed like it would never end. It was like time would stretch out in front of him forever and he would be stuck there with a dry mouth and hunger so deep that he knew it was there, even though his brain tried to block the sensation.

When he finally saw what appeared to be an exit, he half expected the terror to block his path, feign at eating him or do anything to obstruct him. Instead, it laughed out two words. "So curious."

Earwig froze, waiting for the monster to make its play, letting the minutes stretch into an unbearable eternity between each step, half expecting each step to be his last. If it were to attack, what would he do? What could he do against a beast of such unimaginable immensity? For whatever reason, it did not attack and so, one slow step after another, Earwig found himself at the doorway to a dark nexus in another world.

Chapter 16

The Dark Kingdom

The mountains, valleys, and even some of the trees were as he remembered but where the manure-paved roads and earthen huts once stood, was an expansive construction of enormous buildings. Some were so tall that they seemed to touch the sky itself. His eyes were flooded with electric lights and the roads were made of some sort of stone. There was not a barn, stable garden or even a goat to be seen as far as he looked. Instead, there were automobiles. The air had a different smell too. Breathing it stung his lungs and made his eyes water at first but the further he walked, the more he seemed to grow accustomed to or even forget the harsh aspects. Large chimneys billowed clouds of white and black into the sky and a yellow mist hung low in the air. Even with all of the things that had changed, he could see hills that he remembered rolling down as a child.

He hadn't been in the world for five minutes when a truck screeched to a halt behind him. The horn blasted and from inside the cab, a voice called out to him. A man was declaring that he was a part of his anatomy he clearly wasn't and demanding him to "get out of the road!" The driver swerved around him and accelerated, waving at him with one finger held high. A signal that was clearly not meant in any kind respect. Even the castle had changed. It had always been huge but in this world, it sprouted upward and outward to a degree that seemed almost unfathomable, as though the king wanted to show up the very mountains themselves. Signs flashed words. Lightboxes flashed pictures of the king with the words, "**Wanted Dead or Alive**."

He walked away from the enormous building that stood where his doublewide once sat. He knew what he would find inside. Someone that wore his father's face but judging by the high fences and tall judging marble statues, this wasn't his father.

Another automobile screeched to a halt. He could smell its tires melting from the friction of the stop against the pavement. "You trying to get yourself killed!" the sole occupant shouted. "Walking down the middle of the road is a good way to make it happen!"

Earwig didn't respond. Back home he had always walked down the middle of the road. Why else would they have roads if they weren't meant to be traveled on?

"Are you a moron or something," the driver screeched. "Use the damn sidewalk!" He was gesturing to a smaller raised road that ran alongside the wider one. The driver cursed, swerved around him and continued on his way. Earwig crossed over to the sidewalk. The automobiles of this world weren't like the goat carts he was used to but as a nexus keeper he understood their functionality. Everyone was in a hurry to be anywhere else. They were more annoyed than concerned about the fact that he wound up in their way. There were rules to this world that he didn't understand. He would have to learn these rules and fast, before he could even begin to understand why the thread had led him to this world.

First rule, avoid walking on the road. Okay. Second rule: while the cloak made him invisible to the monster, the people here could still see him. He watched the boxes flashing out warnings about smog levels and messages about alerting authorities if you saw King Henesy, who was apparently wanted for treason and was to be considered extremely dangerous. Another message was reminding people that gifting day was resuming soon. Requests should be made to the nexus keeper by no later than Wednesday.

Now the picture on the light box changed to someone who looked like him being trapped by giant metallic gold tentacles, being impaled by fangs, and then shoved into the toothy beak of this world's monster. The words beneath read, *"Nexus Keeper in training executed for treason. Earwigregalus Yohonamonstavitchnic was found guilty of treason after declaring that he would no longer deliver slaves, citing that he had moral apprehension to the practice of human ownership."*

The screen flashed to the picture of a small red headed girl with a strange silver collar on her neck. She was smiling for the camera but there was also a hint of terror behind that awkward smile. Behind her, a family sat around a diner table all staring downward at devices in their hands. This time it was Earwig who cursed, remembering what his grandmother had said about this monster delivering people what they want but do not need. In this world, those deliveries apparently included other people.

Another story flashed onto the screen, *"Mandatory sentences for gifting protestors increased from one to three generations due to an uptick in protest."*

Earwig clenched his jaw. He had delivered books and medication, he had delivered electric lamps, but this other him had delivered people. The next scene showed the man that he knew he would find, in the place where his house should have been. This other father was standing behind a trailer that looked as though it was made for animals but it was filled with people. All of them wore those strange metal collars and chains around their feet and ankles. Behind him, three knights appeared to be counting the passengers. He could see rows of automobiles, televisions, and other items that he didn't know the name of but he understood, the way he understood gifts from his world.

These things were meant to be tools of murder. Like arrows that didn't have to be drawn or reloaded one at a time. Or devices where just pulling a tiny lever could create an explosion that would propel projectiles forward. There were cases of alcohol and piles of clear baggies filled with powders of various colors and grains. All of them intended to make people feel whatever way they wanted to feel. All of them were addictive. There were stacks of coins. More than he had ever seen and his nexus keeper's extra sense told him that this coin was going to someone who already had a fortune.

Everyone here thought he was dead, he realized. His mind locked onto that, so he turned his hood down, away from the screens, away from the road. This was lesson three, his face wasn't safe here.

The smell of something savory led him farther into town, down streets and alleys until he saw three ragged-looking men standing over a burning barrel. Two of them passed a paper bag back and forth while the third tended to what looked like something that used to be an animal. Perhaps a cat, cooking on a stick. He was hungry and thirsty but afraid to show his face. So he stayed back in the shadows, watching and anticipating the hope of food and drink somehow but also sure that it was a hope he would have to abandon. Eventually, hunger won out and he inched forward until the man with the animal on a stick nodded in his direction and his companions turned their heads. One of them smiled, it was genuine but nervous.

"Hope you're not fixing to call the guards on us?" the man asked.

"No," Earwig answered. "I don't think that would be good for me."

"Son of a bitch!" the man who was cooking called out as he got a good look at the boy. His hands pulled through his matted beard. "I know who you are but you're dead. That monster ate you! We all…son of a bitch!" He pointed his finger towards Earwing and his voice and gestures got frantic, but also seemed to betray amiability. "Come here."

As Earwig stepped forward, the three mens eyes widened, half in amazement, half in fear.

"You eat, boy?" the cook asked.

Earwig shook his head.

"I don't think he remembers, boss," said the bearded man who had spoken earlier. The shorter bald guy with a bottle shook his head as well.

"Don't matter," the cook said. "I remember." he tapped a scar on the side of his neck where two lines formed the rough shape of one of the collars that the slaves were wearing.

After waiting for a response the cook pulled the cat off of the stick he was cooking it on. He broke off a leg and handed it to Earwig. Any revulsion he may have had days before was replaced by the size of the void in his stomach and he greedily sunk his teeth in. It was the best thing he had ever tasted. He washed the cat down with the liquid from the flask. It wasn't water. It was bitter and harsh. It made his face feel warm and numb. It seemed to loosen his tongue as well and as the night went on he told the men his story and Leroy the cook shared his in return.

CHAPTER 17

JACK, LENNY, AND LEROY

"My name is Leroy. Once a long long time ago I was a blacksmith. I made a pretty good run at it too but about twenty or so years ago. It seems like people quit relying on other people. The rift grew and the gifts started pouring out and people were able to request damn near anything they wanted. I don't even know how plastic is made but seems everything now is plastic of one type or another. It got so bad, I couldn't even sell nails anymore. Being lean wouldn't have been so bad had I been able to take another job but at some point, people quit hiring people for regular jobs. We went to an indentured economy. Do you know what indentured means?"

Earwig shook his head.

Leroy stretched his massive body twisting his spine one way and then another. After a chain of pops, he moved onto his shoulders and fingers, before continuing. "They don't like us using the *S* word but pretty much we were slaves that sold ourselves. The person that bought me was a shopkeeper by the name of Frank Barley. He fed me a bowl of muck in the morning, one in the afternoon and he kept me up in an old chicken coop. I signed on for five years. In the end, I was supposed to get a whole heap of money. Thousands of coins, enough to set myself up for life. I built stuff and fixed cars, cleaned toilets, whatever. For those first five years, I didn't mind but my term came to an end and Frank said, no. According to him, I still owed him another three years because he hadn't accounted for wear and tear on the coop, the cost of hay, and some tools I broke along the way.

"I let it slide for about a month but every time he came up with a new reason to keep me indentured longer, it was like a kick in the tenders. The last straw was when he had me up patching his roof and I'm baking in the sun. I ask him for a glass of water and he brings it to me but he comes up the ladder with his damn clipboard and adds that to my tab. He didn't say a word, just showed me the bill before climbing back down and that was it.

I went about my chores that night like normal but when he locked me in the shed instead of letting me fall asleep... I shut off my lights and waited, staring through a hole in the wall. When his lights go out I wait some more, two maybe three hours until I'm sure and I push that damn door right off the hinges and pay Mr. Frank a visit.

He may have been bold when he had a pistol and a whip or when he was showing me the bill but when my hands were wrapped around his neck, he was a whole lot more amenable to negotiation. I tied him up good and tight and I go to his safe using the combination he told me. Turned out, Sam didn't have enough coin to his name to melt into a tack, let alone the ten thousand pieces he owed me.

I could have just left, maybe I should have but I needed the coin. I only wanted what I was owed. Some sort of barter to make the last five years of my life worthwhile. When I get to his room though, the guy is untied and he runs after me with a sword. I only hit him once. Once was enough though and he fell flat on his back, stone dead. Two days later the king's guard catches me. They put this collar on my neck and I tried to resist at first but they hurt, those things they put on you. You can't do nothing against them. They don't even have to push a button, they just tell you what to do and the second you think about doing otherwise, it sets all of your nerves ablaze at once. I'm used to getting burned pretty regular-like, but not like this.

*So there it was. I was what they called terminally indentured. They say for three generations. So if I were to have any children or grandchildren they'd be property of the crown. I didn't have any kids but they roomed me up with a few different women and forced us to, you know, try."

There was a long pause. "So we did, we didn't want to but we did. I guess I might have a seed out there somewhere but they sold me before I ever found out. That guy tried to get some selling stock from me and then he sold me.

So the rich types sell me back and forth for years and then one day we get sent to the Nexus cause another rich jerk wished for more slaves.

I met Jack and Lenny there. We were packed so tight in a stock trailer that you couldn't sit down. Jack here couldn't talk. Rumor is that he was a city guard but he got caught publishing a flier against indenturing people. And Lenny ..." Leroy paused and looked over to the heavier-built bearded man next to him.

"It's ok," Lenny said but Leroy waited.

"Let's just say I was a lot like Frank but I didn't have enough money to pay the taxes I owed."

"Yeah he almost got let out of his servitude early by some people he swindled but I didn't feel like sharing my spot on the trailer floor with a corpse. Long story short, I had just gotten done with a bit of a scuffle when we ran into a kid with a face just like yours. He puts a little box next to our collars, presses a button and the damn thing falls off. We were all standing around in a trailer stinking of our excrement. Slave after slave, he breaks the bonds then opens the gate to the trailer and runs off into the night. It takes us a long time, almost too damn long to comprehend what being free really meant but eventually we start to leave. One person, then another, and another. Until all three hundred of us are scattering this way and that.

They put TV's up all over the place and they filmed that monster ripping that kid apart just so they could force us to see. We all saw that. We saw the video of him getting caught. They pounded the blazes out of that kid. It was hard to watch but we did and we noticed what they didn't find. They didn't find his machine.

I don't know how many of us are left. I reckon the guards caught quite a few by now. They ain't got us all though and that's all that matters. There's more slaves in this world than the people who keep us. If we can find that machine and make more like it..." Leroy sighed then looked at his partners.

"Time to move," he finished. Then he looked at Earwig. "You might be a bigger find than the box but I won't make you do anything you're not comfortable with. Still if enough people see you… I gotta believe that there's still good in this world."

They moved from the alleyways to the gutters beneath the street. Walking through the perpetual stream of dank foul water until they found an intersection of dry pipes. They all chose a pipe to sleep in before removing their wet socks and boots. They hung them up in the hopes that they would dry a little overnight. Earwig followed suit before laying down for the most uncomfortable but inevitable slumber of his life.

He woke up much later but found he was still awake before the others and so he pulled out his mirror to see what it could tell him of these three men. When he looked at Jack, the reflection was of the guard that let him escape into the nexus of his own world. His face looked nothing like the other man's. This guy was short and bald but something in the eyes still matched.

When he looked at Leroy he saw Leroy almost exactly as he was but understood that there was more to it. He was half glass, half steel with deep wounds and a sadness that he never spoke about. The sadness of Leroy wasn't due to his own losses but due to the fact that he couldn't help but to have empathy for everyone he saw. Even the people he counted as enemies.

When he looked at Lenny, he forced himself to look away. Back farther in his life, before he was indentured himself, he collected slaves by the scores. Slaves to do the shopping, slaves to read to him, and slaves to fight other slaves in the gambling halls. Even other slaves to entertain his every wish and whim. As if that wasn't enough, he barely allowed his slaves enough food and water. He never let his slaves see a doctor or take a day off. Which meant he had slaves burying slaves. Slaves that he allowed to die.

When he had more time with Leroy alone, Earwig pressed the issue. "He was bad, you know, real bad."

"Yeah, he was." Leroy agreed.

"Do you trust him?" Earwig asked.

"It's not a matter of trust. He's likely to drown with us if he tries to sink this boat. I do need to know something though." Leroy sighed, "I need to know if someone like him, now that he's been on both sides… I need to know if he can change? If he can be as he ought? I need him to change because if he can't, if he hasn't, what's the point? If I can find a way to free people but they keep on making more slaves, which they will… It has to count for something. It only counts if I can change the minds of people like him. He might betray me. He might find a way to sell me down the river and get back to his comfortable life but if that happens, if I'm worth that much, then it means I'm doing something right. But he might also surprise me. He might stick his neck out or take a risk and prove to me once and for all that those people can change. So he's here at my right-hand side and that's all I'm going to say on that subject."

Chapter 18

Revolution Part 1

This was so much bigger than Earwig could handle. Somewhere on the opposite of the Nexus, in a different universe, his father was sick, perhaps dying or perhaps dead. The mirror wasn't showing him anything useful when he held his fathers picture up to it, it was flashing back memories. He needed medicine, strong medicine and to find whatever mysterious aspect it was that grandmother had him searching for. Something of her to love, but this wasn't her world.

The monster here was feeding off the opposite stuff, which explained why it was so much bigger. It fed when people created injustice. It fed when people fought injustice. It fed when people got used to instant gratification and had to wait even seconds to get what they wanted. It fed when they were mistrusting or scared and it feasted when they were so accustomed to the cruelty that they became indifferent. It was shocking the first time he saw the darkness enveloping people as they walked past the slaves but it made sense.

His monster fed off love. He had always assumed that hate was the opposite of love. It wasn't though, because in order to hate you still had to care on some level. So the feedings the beast got from angry words, a fight or even a murder were nothing in comparison to the feedings it got from the people who could watch these things, just walk on by and be happy that they weren't involved.

They spent most of the next week in the gutters. He came out three times to rummage through the city streets or the forest in hopes of finding the other Earwig's machine or to score a quick meal by chance, be it a rat or stray dog. When they found those meals, no matter what sort of critter it was, Leroy was the one who took care of the hard part. He always did it in private but Earwig and the others could hear him apologizing to it before a loud crack from his stick silenced the noise, saving a few of Leroy's sniffles.

His eyes always seemed to glisten as though he had been hurt himself but he never said a word about it. He just cooked it up and tried to smile, while Lenny and Jack passed around a flask. He found a different flask that he filled with water to share with Earwig. He didn't let Earwig drink from the other flask after that first day. "Sorry kid, it's just not right for a kid to be drinking that stuff."

On a few occasions, they ran into other acquaintances from the night of their escape. Every time they did, it was Leroy that did the talking. Lenny and Jack tucked themselves away into a corner. While nobody ever had a problem with Jack, Earwig could see the glares they gave Lenny.

For his part, Lenny often tried to look the other way. He didn't say much on the subject because he knew that somehow Earwig wasn't comfortable with him but on one occasion, when some particularly strong abuse was being directed at the whole group, he apologized to Earwig.

"None of you deserve this. I deserve it all though. I was a monster and I deserve everything that I have coming. I'd leave but I know without the big guy, I'd be dead within a day. I should go but…" he sighed, "I'm a coward. I'm not ready to die." He fell silent for quite a time then whispered to himself. "I'll get over that though. Just you watch."

He didn't speak about it again for quite some time. His musings were interrupted by Leroy cursing loudly.

"The good news is about two hundred of us are still free. The bad news is nobody's seen the box, not in the woods, not near the river, not in the gutters. It's just gone."

"We're not going to find that box unless the monster wants us to," Earwig spoke up. I don't know why I didn't realize it sooner. "There's a story from my world about our king getting angry at the Kindness after his friend died and crushing a spider. To warn him, the beast covered his entire castle in webbing. All of the guards were stuck in place. It hoisted giant stone tables to the ceiling. The octopuses filled up every river and every well. The forests themselves were covered in black masses of spiders. Steel doors were consumed by mushrooms and everything near the king crumbled to the touch.

That was her warning. If I wanted to hide something, I would have hidden it in my house. Even then, if the monster in my world didn't want me to have it, there wouldn't be any place I could hide it where she wouldn't see it. They move in a space that we can't even imagine, the same as if we could move above a bug on the floor without it noticing us."

"But he built that thing, he freed us right under the monster's nose!" Larry countered.

"The monster was okay with it," Earwig answered. "The beast isn't on one side or another. It's feeding on anger, hate, fear, and indifference; mostly indifference. You're all out here taking care of yourselves in small groups. The people you got away from are madder than hornets. The debate you sparked is giving a lot of people the chance to ignore the subject for fear of seeming too political or radical. No matter what the outcome is, it feeds.

The problem is there isn't a damn thing we can do to fight it. Only your king can, and only after he passes his thousand-year test. If he fails the test but still kills the beast, he will become a Terror himself but instead of just living here and feeding off of all the ugliness, he would destroy this world and find another world or perhaps many other worlds to torment. My king is taking the same test." Earwig paused, absorbing the stares of his companions for several seconds. "There is another way but it's risky. We give the beast what it wants. Chaos, real chaos."

Earwig spun towards a shadow to his right. "If you allow it, let my grandmother feed a little here in this world. The same way you are feeding in mine. Bring your weapons from the Nexus, flood the streets outside of all of the slave owner's houses, and let me get the things I need to build a device that sets the slaves free, all of them. I know what will happen, it doesn't suit me but maybe a little darkness is necessary from time to time. The point is, you will feast for a long, long time after that and you'll get to watch me suffer the consequences."

There was a sudden rush of pattering feet followed by silence.

"I don't understand. What just happened?" Leroy asked, incredulous.

"The king in my world is the flip side of the king in yours. The monsters believe that both kings will either turn into Terrors or that one of them will turn into a Kindness and the other a Terror but I don't believe that anymore. My world is ruled by the Kindness and everything still got dismal. This world is ruled by the Terror, and yet you took me in. You took in Lenny and looked after him. You fought for him even knowing his past. Sorry Lenny, what you did doesn't deserve forgiveness but maybe, maybe something you do in the future will. I can't say.

What I'm planning to do will make everything bad, real bad for a really long time but maybe I was looking at it wrong the whole time. Maybe the Kindness isn't always the answer. Maybe the Terror isn't always wrong. What man does to other men, or for them, they would do that no matter what monster rules their realm.

So I'm starting a war. It will likely be long and terrible, all of the things your monster loves. When it's done people will be bitter about it for a long time but it's also for the greater good. At least I hope it will be. Do I have your support?"

Leroy nodded but swallowed in slow apprehension. He had just witnessed a deal with the monster and from what he knew about those sorts of deals, there was always a twist. For his part, Earwig seemed to know what the twist was going to be and that was enough for him. Tens of thousands of slaves were being released in a city where there were maybe half that number of slave owners and a handful of bystanders.

"It may be less of a war and more of a bloodbath. If they got serious about going after Lenny, I wouldn't be able to protect him."

Lenny looked back at Earwig. "I know you don't trust me and you shouldn't but if you could think of any way I could help? I do want to help. I want to do one thing right and then I'm going to accept it or at least I'm going to try. I don't want you to save me this time Leroy, Not you, either Jack. I owe so much more to the people who will be coming for me than I do to the king. There's no way I can ever pay it back but a bunch of them have already named their price. In my head, I'm ok with it. I'm scared and I'm afraid I might try to betray you tomorrow when it feels real but if you can think of a way today, I want to help."

That night as the others slept tucked into their drainpipes, Earwig lay down, eyes half closed, waiting for a feeling that he knew all too well. When he felt it, he woke up to find giant boxes, wires, speakers, and screws. As well as screwdrivers, pliers, and tools. All he had to do was touch the items and something inside took over. His nexus keeper's gift. He knew how everything fit together, why and where. By the time the others awoke, the machine was assembled and ready to go. Unfortunately, they weren't awoken under natural circumstances but by the tip of a guard's sword. Everyone except Lenny. He had slipped away as Earwig pretended to sleep. He thought about stopping him but didn't know if what he was planning had as much to do with the monster's will as anything he could have planned. So he found himself collared, along with his friends and loaded in the back of a truck, machine in tow, bound for the Nexus.

It was storming that morning, hard. Lightning arched across the overcast sky, making strange patterns as the darkness swallowed it and seemed to intercept mid-arch, casting an almost imperceivable shadow across the kingdom.

"I can't believe he betrayed us," Leroy lied. He knew Lenny would. He knew it was the best time for it to happen in order to save his own skin. Yet somehow, somewhere deep in his heart, he felt like the time they spent together (the time that Lenny survived under Leroy's protection) could have counted for something. The black glow of the Nexus seemed to shine darkness right through their souls. "Would it have worked? Did you finish?" Leroy asked.

Earwig nodded and half a second later both Leroy and Jack were convulsing and screaming. The screaming continued for almost half an hour as they both tried to overcome the pain and willing themselves to the bright switches.

Earwig shook his head. This was never going to go according to plans. At least not his. He could plan for what to do over the course of days, weeks, months or years but the monster could plan for centuries. His singular hope was that their interest aligned enough for some short-term win. However, it was no use telling his companions that. Leroy had become single-minded about ending internment. He could tell by the looks in Jack's eyes that he shared that conviction but without the naive frivolous hope.

What did Earwigregalus believe though? He believed that the monster had provided the exact tools he needed for him to make a device that would release all of the slaves at once. He believed, judging by the looks of it, that Macrothele had delivered weapons to more strange places in one night than he had ever delivered before. When they arrived at the trailer there was an army of guards waiting for them, alongside Macrothele and none other than Lenny himself.

"You son of a bitch! You son of a bitch. I'll kill you!" Leroy howled. Lenny frowned, turning away from the carriage and towards the guard who handed him a paper pardon and a purse full of coins.

He turned again with the purse in hand, looking at his former friend. "I'm sorry. I had to. It was the only way."

The back of the carriage opened. A guard hollered into a larger trailer that was also opening. "All of you, just stay right where ye are until this door closes again!"

"I had to," Lenny shouted again, this time with a little smile. "It was the only way to get his machine to the Nexus!" He pulled the remote Earwig had given him out of his pocket, his thumb already on the button. From the back of the trailer the machine hummed to life and screamed out a screech that made everyone drop to their knees. As the collars fell clanking to the ground Lenny crawled towards the trailer still calling, "I'm sorry!"

Earwig balked. "This wasn't the plan. Lenny was supposed to get away first. He could have pressed the button from the forest. That would have at least given him enough time to try and hide but instead he pushed himself into the trailer with all of the former slaves, where his friends were helpless to stop the forward march of hundreds of angry people. They managed to clear the door but Lenny just lay there, apologizing as the fists, clawed hands and rocks all came tumbling down on him.

Earwig remembered Lenny saying that they had already named their price but that part of his friend's contrition he had been unconvinced of until now. Lenny was dead and hundreds of slaves poured out of the trailer. Behind them thousands more poured out of the house, all of them taking up arms. This world's Macrothele retreated into the Nexus, where nobody dared follow. The guards put up a meager attempt at fighting but even the best-trained guard could only cut down three or four men before scores more fell over top of them.

All across the kingdom, the same story was playing out: explosions, riots, fire, and murder. It was a balking orgy of carnage but even as the darkness swelled across the sky, something else came into the world in the form of a voice that Earwig knew well. A voice that his friends didn't hear. "What did you do?" grandmother asked.

"He's feeding in our world. You need to feed here. There's more love, more kindness, and hope than you know." He didn't answer her question. He didn't feel it deserved an answer. Nothing could convince him that the right thing to do was always the good thing. This was gross and messy but also important.

Chapter 19

The Things You Get Used To.

Earwig had hoped that righting the huge wrong he saw would somehow lead to the end of his trip to the dark kingdom. It didn't. If anything, it may have set him back. Things didn't get better like he hoped they would, but somehow inside, he knew they wouldn't.

There were fires, explosions and screams every night. Sometimes it was former slaves, sometimes it was the people who had claimed to own them. He spent the first week thinking that he would never get used to it. He did; however, get used to seeing the horrors of wars, to violence, to fighting, to death, and worst of all to keeping his head down and looking away so that he didn't attract trouble.

He wasn't just used to it. It was a relief. He didn't have to live in the shadows as he once did before. As long as he didn't have a gas bomb in his hands, the guards could have cared less about him, no matter whose face he wore. It would be weeks before the riots settled down. The spike in murders continued for some months after that but it didn't matter. Some of the storefronts that survived the initial bloodbath and the new storefronts which popped up in the aftermath, no longer used indentured servants. People got paid for the time they worked and after they were done they went home. The owners, most of whom were considered new rich, insisted on it.

Signs of his grandma were also making their appearance, edible mushrooms, books on healing, gifts that people needed more than wanted. Earwig hoped that it would both give her strength and maybe protect him from the wrath of the Terror, once the chaos he started had settled out. It was hard to know for certain because she was more of a hands off style of monster. At least she was getting some sustenance here now. He had to hope that would help his father back home, somehow.

As the weeks turned into months, the chaos shifted into an uneasy and suspicious peace. The guard's eyes turned back towards him. They hadn't forgotten about the resurrected son of a nexus keeper. The ghost that crashed their entire economy. The guards didn't go right for him. They couldn't because he was now part folk hero, part legend and taking him in broad daylight would have probably started another riot.

Instead, they sent plain-clothed guards to stalk him. He started seeing the same people every morning when he woke up and left his apartment. They would follow him throughout the day and even at night as he searched with the mirror, desperate to find some thread, or piece of a magic puzzle that would allow him to go back home.

CHAPTER 20

ANOTHER DEAL

One day, when he was returning from his millionth fruitless trip. The din of conflict had faded. Instead of rations and exit plans, people were busy arguing about whether it was a Tuesday, a Wednesday, or some other day altogether. Shops with boarded-up windows announced, *"Come in, we're actually open."* Custodians swept glass and debris and the city guards stood watching and smiling, greeting people like nothing had ever happened.

Earwig could feel the eyes on him. This uneasy peace was good for the people but he knew that the longer it lasted the more danger he was in. So he took to the alleys and sewers again, doing his best to keep out of everyone's view.

It didn't work. There were always people. Circling, watching and shifting in ways that made his heart race. They were coming for him. He could feel it. He slunk from one dark narrow alley to the next so often that even his supernatural sense of direction felt inverted. Then it happened.

He heard a step. A shadow darker than the one he was hiding in shifted. Something large and soft fell over his face. He writhed in defiance but the hand only tightened. He tried to scream, tried to turn to fight, to do anything but the figure who captured him was almost as tall as Leroy and held him with such a fierce grip that every effort felt moot.

It pulled him deep into an alley. He tried to kick, to squirm, punch and bite but the spector held him tight. The figure resisted every ounce of energy Earwig spent to escape it.

"If you scream, we're both dead," came the voice finally. He remembered that voice from a distant lifetime ago. The hand released and his body was spun around so that his eyes met and locked with the eyes of this world's King Henesy.

"Philip's goons were going to kill you tonight," he announced. They have a new collar that they are dying to test out on me but you, they just want you dead. They know that as a nexus keeper you could break that collar anytime you want to. By the end of the week they are going to start rounding up slaves again, not all of them, just some key figures to make an example out of. It will work of course. Until the beast gets hungry for chaos again."

"Still, you played chess with a god and if only for a couple of moves, you had it in check. We have a mutual friend that was both impressed and horrified by that. More horrified, if I'm being honest. She has trouble understanding the darkness, the way our monster has trouble seeing the light. I tried to explain, the best I could."

The king pulled him deeper and deeper into the alley before tapping on a wooden door three times, then six and then eleven times. Each grouping was followed by a pause, then repeated twice more. A shadow crossed the door and waited for a few seconds before it cracked open.

On the other side, a person who was almost Nancy waited three steps back, sword drawn. "You got him."

"Yeah, but the little bugger bit me," Henesy said with a faint smile. He showed her the bloody wound on his hand and she winced.

"No matter. He's safe." This world's version of Nancy replied. Had it not been for the fierceness in her eyes, Earwig wouldn't have been able to tell. In this world, she was a fighter.

"We can talk freely now. Nancy here has made friends with our mutual friend. She has enough love in her heart to keep the Terror away.

Anyhow, I'm sure that you know about the deal I made. Your king made one too. So I'll cut to the chase. You brought hope to our kingdom. You brought hope in truckloads and you tricked the Terror into delivering you everything you needed to bring that hope.

Sure he got the feast he was promised but after the feast, we could feel it. The whole damn world was different. It wasn't as dark as it was before and even if they start making slaves again… it will never be the same. You knew that would happen didn't you?

"No," Earwig answered, "but I hoped it would."

"How?" the king asked.

Earwig frowned. "I don't know if grandma will like my answer. He took a breath. I used to think that they were good and bad. One was all good and one was all bad but it's not like that. The Kindness doesn't create the love. The Terror doesn't create the hate, fear, and apathy.

They're more like gardeners. They are trying to grow what's already there. People were mad at the injustice and that's a good thing. They should be mad, even hateful towards those who trap and abuse other people. It's the right thing to feel.

I knew it and the Terror knew it. So I made a deal with the monster to let grandmother in here. So there could be hope alongside all of the hate. In return, I started a war. I don't know if grandma can understand that. Sometimes, fighting is the answer. Sometimes, the right thing to do and the good thing to do are not always the same."

"I don't know if that helps me," the king replied. "When I face the Terror... If I kill it... I have to do so without hatred and bitterness in my heart. I watched that monster tear my wife limb from limb. When my son died and I begged to have him brought back, I knew that it wasn't right but I was torn, so I begged. I begged the thing that I hate.

Philip was a hundred when he died. When the beast gave him back to me, he looked no more than thirty years old. I wanted it to be him. I wanted it to be real. It wasn't. The beast put something..," the king looked ashamed.

"At first, I felt terrible for questioning him, like the worst father in the world but he passed by his bakery without even looking twice, without smelling the air. All of his natural life he used to smile at babies. He used to pet every dog or goat in his path. He used to spend hours looking for the perfect flowers to lay on his wife's grave.

All of that was gone. This thing with my son's face was now obsessed with power, politics, immortality, his ascension, ending crime, and expanding the kingdom. My boy hated all of those things. This thing spoke of nothing else.

Then one day there was a man caught stealing bread. I didn't have the heart to execute him. I was over it. All of it. Just as I told the guards to let him go, Philip marched in. He just wrapped his hands around this guy's neck and squeezed.

The look in Philip's eyes, as the guy squirmed and fought, it was like a kid with a stack of presents. He was so happy, as happy as I'd ever seen him in his life, watching that man die. I yelled for him to stop but he just kept squeezing, harder and harder, his face twisting with some evil joy. When he dropped the man's body, he turned to me and pulled the crown right off of my head.

"You're no king, father," he said. "You make me sick."

" I could tell by his expression and by the guards' reactions, it was over. I wasn't a king anymore, so I ran.

This Philip doesn't care about bread. He doesn't care about his former wife or anything of that sort. He craves power, power, and immortality. He wants to become a Terror. Which he can do if he executes me when my thousand years run out. Then he can drink my blood and challenge the beast himself."

"Would you like some zucchini bread hun," Nancy interrupted. She placed a warm slice of bread in Earwig's hand and smiled. "I had to make a little something when I knew we were going to have company." She left the room and returned two seconds later with a glass of milk.

"I'd like some bread and milk too," Henesy said with a fake whimper in his voice.

"You're a grown man, you can get it your damn-self but not before I fix up that hand."

"My dad?" Earwig interjected. He had wanted to ask so many times before but he couldn't. Even now as the words hung in the air and he waited to hear grandma's voice (which she would attempt to make as comforting as possible) he was bracing himself, getting ready for all of the wind to get knocked out of his soul.

"He is still with us. He sleeps but is getting stronger," Grandmother answered.

The relief he felt was short-lived. Was that good news or bad news? It had been so long since he entered the Nexus under horrendous circumstances. His father was alive, yes but if he was going to get better, he should have come around by now.

"He is getting stronger," she said.

He clamped down on his worry. It wouldn't do him any good here. If he was going to save his dad he needed to keep his wits about him. He needed to focus on the task at hand and find whatever it was he was looking for that would help him reconnect to the Kindness.

He took a deep breath and spoke to Henesy again. "I don't know if I can help you the way that you want me to help. I got so mad and resentful that I broke my Nexus. Try as I might, I can't force myself to think the way that I know I should be thinking. I shouldn't be able to see the purpose in the darkness but I can't help but see how, sometimes, not always, but sometimes it's the right path. The Kindness, it's sweet but it's not always effective. Maybe that's why she sent me here, so I could witness how horrible it is but I can't help it. My heart is walking in both worlds, the way it always has. I'm broken. I know it. I don't think I can be fixed. I'll try to help you, but I'm afraid that I am more likely to let you down."

"What a steaming heap of bovine excrement!" the king declared. Do you know what bovine excrement is?" he asked and answered just as quickly with a common swear word. "You've given people hope, not just wishy-washy hope but actual proof that things can be different! Do you know what I believe? That the hope you brought gives me the best chance I've ever had."

They talked for a while longer and ate countless slices of zucchini bread before Nancy brought over a stack of blankets that smelled like coconuts in the springtime. He buried his nose inside and it made him think about the stink of home and the stink of the sewers. Compared to what he was used to, he did not want to quit smelling the blankets.

She showed him to a room with a cot and whispered in a soft reassuring voice before closing the door. "He's not wrong, you know. What you did for all of those people, that was a really good thing and don't you forget it. It had to be hard, making that call at your age, but you weren't wrong."

She kissed him on the head and then let herself out. He didn't even realize he was crying and couldn't tell how long it had been going on for but he knew that was what he needed to hear. He must have shed a tear for every body he had seen lying in the street after the riots started. For the burnt-out shops, homes, and the children running from the chaos. For the fathers, both on the guards' side and on the slaves' side. The ones that never got to go home and for the forgiveness that Lenny never asked for, nor received, whether he deserved it or not. When the tears finally stopped flowing, he fell asleep and he felt peaceful for the first time since he had arrived in this dark world.

The next morning he was woken up to the pattern being pounded hard against the door, followed by the sound of a murmuring scream. It was Jack. When the door was opened he faced Nancy frantically dancing his hands in the air.

"Woa, slow down there, you know I'm not that fast," she insisted. But Jack's shaking hands continued dancing until Nancy screamed out the worst curse she knew. She turned to Earwig. "They caught Leroy. They are holding him at the Nexus. If you don't turn yourself in by tomorrow morning..." She didn't finish, she didn't have to. they all heard the loud deep rasping voice of the Terror as he laughed.

"Do you want to make a deal? I do so miss your brand of chaos. I might even let you live if you can make it worth my while again."

"Don't," Nancy warned, but Earwig was already walking in circles. His head awash in adrenaline, plans, and fears. If he showed up there and died, (perhaps with or perhaps without his friends) it would feed the beast. If he didn't show up there, they would come here. Grandma may have had her feelers in this world now but the Terror was making a show to prove to him that this was still very much his world. Earwig didn't doubt that.

"It has to be worth my while to, Monster."

"Funny," the monster laughed. "I didn't feel you pushing a wheelbarrow in front of you when you crossed my web. How'd you manage to take those great big balls of gaul along without tripping all over them."

"Are our goals so incompatible? I want justice and freedom. You want chaos. There is room for those two things to intersect."

"What the hell are you doing?" Henesy scolded.

"He'll get what he wants whether I cooperate or not. If I refuse there'll be guards knocking down every door and crashing through every window by noon," Earwig snapped back.

"We can't fight him, it would be like fighting the sun or the sea, or both. There's no way to stop him, not in the traditional sense. We either let him take us and kill us as he will or we try to make some good come out of this. After he gets what he wants, he'll just come back for you again and again and again. You're going to become what you are trying to fight. What I've been trying to fight for almost a thousand years!"

"That is the crux of it, ain't it? He's going to get what he wants. I'm inclined to help him but only if the fight I pick is worth fighting for. I don't want to play this game forever."

"Careful now, your willingness to play this game is the one reason I have kept you alive." the monster scoffed.

Grandmother's voice broke into the room. "I cannot bring you home yet, but I may be able to take you away."

"Maybe," Earwig answered. "But not yet. If the people thought I died, would you let me leave?" He asked the Terror.

"It is all the same to me." It lied.

"And my friends, if I promise to come back before I go home? If I promise one last sensation, one last feast, but a cause attached to it. Would they be kept under your protection and grandma's watch."

"Do tell," the Terror hissed.

"I save Leroy, with the king and a few friends at my side but the people see me die. Before I'm gone, I shout out that *I'll be back*. The king declares slavery to be illegal and decrees Philip's reign is illegitimate, though it won't stop the guards from trying to apprehend him. My friends get some assistance fighting their way into the shadows where they disappear."

"The castle is very well armed. If you pit the castle against the kingdom, lots of innocent people will die. All that anger. All that grief. I'm sure to be exploding by the time you return."

"Promise," Earwig barked back.

"I promise, that if you do not pass through this world on your way home, no one in the history of life will have ever endured a slower and more excruciating death than that of your friends. But...yes, go ahead and make your plans. Save Leroy and when you see the hell I make of this plan of yours, you can spend the rest of your life toiling over how it would have been easier and more noble to just die." When the Terror's voice finally died down, they all stood gazing at each other in horrified silence.

"I'm sorry I included you guys in this. It's not like it was before, even though it was messy, it felt right. I'm not sure I wasn't just trying to save my own ass here. I don't know if I did the right thing."

The king placed his hand on Earwig's shoulder. "Chin up. It's hard to make a good deal with the devil when there's a pitchfork sticking in your ass."

Chapter 21

A Sideways Plan

This time there were no fancy machines that his mind supernaturally grasped. No armor or no outsiders helping. The only pieces of equipment he found were two clear plastic shields that scrambled vertical but not horizontal light. They were tall and lean, allowing him to hold one at his side and walk down the street beside a building without anyone seeing. As long as they didn't look too hard.

Behind him, the king followed and so it was that they inched their way from the hideout to the town square, where anchors waited. Swordsmen were posted on roof tops and by most of the alleyways. In the stocks, at the very center, Leroy sat waiting for the posted axman to receive the orders that would end his life.

Leroy smiled, his eyes twinkled and he kept on shouting that it was worth it, mixing various profanities in with the statement from time to time. On the edges, between the guards and where the king and Earwig stood, were crowds of villagers. They had their own swords, knives and trash can lids.

Everyone knew the second the axe fell that the whole damn city was about to burn. The breadth of the city held, and then it happened. A man and a child, just sort of appeared out of nowhere. They strode across the square and while the man squared off with the guard holding the axe, the child used a wire to open the shackles and set the giant of a man free.

It was at that moment that the confusion about their appearance turned to elation and the crowd seemed to boil over. A thick volley of arrows rained down but every damn one of them missed.

Henesy shouted to tempestuous applause. "SLAVERY IS AN ABOMINATION! AS YOUR KING, I HEREBY DECREE THAT HOLDING ANOTHER PERSON IN SERVITUDE IS A CRIME OF THE WORST DEGREE! FURTHERMORE...," more arrows struck the dirt as he continued, "PRINCE PHILIP HAS NO RIGHTS OR PRIVILEGES GRANTED BY THE THRONE! HIS REIGN IS ILLEGAL AND ANYONE STILL SERVING UNDER HIS FALSE CROWN SHALL BE DEALT WITH!"

Only the King and Earwig could see shimmering blue as the rift opened before them. It was time for act three. One final bow before he disappeared in dramatic fashion but Earwig couldn't move. A swarm of spiders had pinned his legs to the ground. Undulating beneath them, a giant golden tentacle shot out, crushing Earwig's torso.

Guards with metal boots, spiked gloves, and chainmail armor rushed in kicking, punching, and even stabbing. He could feel himself breaking, this wasn't just an act. They were going to literally kill him and if that wasn't bad enough he could hear the Terror laughing as the hooks under its tentacle tore into his skin.

"YOU ARROGANT FOOL. YOU DON'T SERVE ME ANYMORE," the beast's voice thundered in Earwig's head.

Henesy's sword sunk deep into the tentacle again and again and again. He broke through the gold plating, covering the ground, himself and Earwig in thick black foul-smelling blood. All at once Earwig was free. He struggled to stand and even struggled to think as Henesy hoisted his body up. The king abandoned his sword and charged forward, throwing Earwig into the rift. Henesy pivoted, turning back around to square off with the monster, its webs already overtaking his body. A new tentacle appeared, twisted around him. There was nothing more he could do, so he turned to Leroy and gasped out, "run!"

That's just what Leroy did. He charged back and the crowd charged forward, defending their hero and king against a god. They were dying in mass but as they did, they eventually freed him from the lashing appendages of the beast.

Out of sight, inside the Nexus, Earwig was left contemplating if this was really all part of the deal. He was hurt as badly as he had ever been, but he knew he wouldn't die, not here. Before the rift could close, he decided that for the sake of his friends, he had better stick with the plan and he half screamed out the words. "I'll be back!" These deals always go sideways.

On the other side of the rift, the monster would have its war. The people would unite with the king against the son-like-being who deposed him.

They would unite against the monster. Earwig would become a martyr, causing many in that crowd to lose all of their good sense. They would hate for him. Hate the man sitting on the throne, the guards, the beast itself, and the nexus keeper.

They would hate and they would die, which would enrage more and more people. It would feed the darkness and when Earwig fulfilled his promise and came back to save his friends, the beast would likely kill him again, for real. This time he wouldn't be returning.

How many people were going to die, for the lives of a few? Hundreds of thousands? All of them? It was overwhelming. He couldn't think about it, he had to move forward. He was in the Nexus now, beyond the Terror's reach for the moment. A more welcome blue-black tentacle and several spider arms appeared and became busy wrapping his wounds in silk and unwrapping skin that had reformed. Broken bones were healed within seconds. The thread he was following before was in his hand again, leading him on towards another door, another world.

He followed it because in spite of what may or may not have been his tremendous missteps in the dark world, his father still needed him and the only way he would be able to help him is by finding whatever it was she had sent him to find. Something to love in her.

He wasn't sure that he would recognize what that was when he found it but he was a nexus keeper, so he had to try.

Chapter 22

Wisconsin

He waited. At the edge of the doorway, for fear of what kind of shadowy world he would step into now. What ancient evils would claim it as theirs? From his perspective, the only clue he could see was a sign that read, *"Welcome to Wisconsin."* There was a cow painted beneath it that looked as though it had known many horrors during its time in this twisted realm. After working up the courage, he stepped out.

He was at the edge of some sort of ocean, dark almost black-blue water matching the overcast sky as it wrapped around most of the world in one direction. On the beach, facing a pier, the horrified cow watched the water. It seemed ever cautious for the elder gods that might slink out in order to torment its mortal soul.

From somewhere further down on the pier a shrill whistle sounded. "Ey you boy! This ain't no public beach. If you ain't riding on the ferry, you need to get. If you ain't accompanied by an adult, ya ain't ridin'." So Git!" The man who shouted made some frantic hand gestures.

Earwig didn't understand half of what the man was talking about but he didn't care either. He just wanted to be somewhere far away from the disturbing gaze of that cow. Far away from that ocean and whatever lurked beneath it. So he obeyed, pressing one foot in front of the other. Crossing around the outside of the chain link fence, he saw another sign that read, "*Lake Michigan Pier.*" He kept going just step after step.

Judging by the sun it was morning time here. At least if the sun worked the same way in this world as it did in his, most people wouldn't be up yet. He crossed another bridge. Underneath, a group of ragged men lay sleeping next to a smothered campfire. Were they refugees? It might be good to know them, or perhaps it might not. The rules of this world were not yet clear but at least he knew how to get out of it.

He walked in the opposite direction of the rising sun throughout the day, night, and well into the next day, leaving the pier and the ocean-sized lake at his back. His nexus keeper instincts were giving him the ability to know something that there was no logical explanation for. They told him that this was the direction that he needed to go. He went from a city to the country, past a few small towns, and back into what appeared to be a larger city.

The first hint that his journey had a purpose and he wasn't just wandering, came when he saw a dark glean in a tree next to another large lake. The green signage here said it was called *Lake Monona*. It was another nexus, not one to his world but a direct line back into the world of the Terror.

He had never seen a dark portal in his world. Nor had he ever seen a light portal in the dark world, save for the rift that was opened up for him when he left.

This was something new. These portals had been here for a long, long time. Perhaps forever but hidden from the sight of people who didn't know what they were looking at.

What did that mean? Did the Terror and the Kindness both operate here? Had they portioned out cites? Did Milwaukee belong to the Kindness and Madison belong to the Terror? It didn't matter. He was meant to see that nexus but he was here for something else right now, whatever that was.

He pressed on until he could smell the grease frying in a nearby restaurant. He understood that if he looked in the garbage bins around the back, there was a chance he might find food but there was something else besides his stomach that carried him here. A feeling of familiarity or comfort. He found his way into the large green bins by popping the tops up one by one to view the only menu he was equipped to order from.

He decided on a round silver foil with the words *Burgerworld* and *Big Buddy* scrawled across the top in giant yellow letters. It smelled better than any of the rats or cats he had been forced to dine on recently.

"Don't eat that," a scalding but familiar voice called out. "I'm sorry for yelling but wait here for ten minutes and I'll get you some food. Just don't eat that. They poison those bins, hun."

It was Nancy, but she was young. In the world that he had just come from, she was in her sixties. Here she looked to be only in her mid-twenties. He was about to say something but he paused. The nexus keeper part of his brain warned him. If he told her all that he had to say now, there was no way she would believe him.

She had to be the reason. The key to why he was here, whether she knew it or not. Maybe she was in some sort of danger? If she worked here, she had to live a lot closer to the Terror.

"Ok," he answered after a pause." I'll wait." She disappeared inside and true to her word, reemerged ten minutes later with two steaming bags and a tall cup. I got you a coke and I wasn't sure whether you were an onion ring guy or not, so I got you a fry and a big buddy that hasn't been laying in rat poison all night." After handing him the bag and the cup, she gave him a little nod and disappeared.

He ate his food and then retreated down the road to a patch of trees where he could sit and watch for her to leave without her knowing. About six hours later, she exited the building. This time instead of the bright yellow shirt and pants, she wore blue jeans and a hoodie. She was carrying about five bags in one hand and in the other hand, she had a cardboard tray with five of the fizzy drinks she had just given him.

She carried them over to an automobile. It was a small black rusty car with rounded corners and the letters *VW* squeezed together on the trunk. Then she pulled out of the lot, heading towards him at first before turning back towards the lake and the dark nexus.

When he saw where she was heading, he crept out from the trees and started to jog. However, her car turned again bypassing the nexus and parked near a bridge, where she carried the baggies to another group of ragged men.

Then she got in her automobile and was gone again. He walked in the direction she had been going but by the time he got to that corner, the *VW* was already a speck on the horizon. With nothing else to do, he walked, hoping to latch on to the same feeling that brought him to her in the first place. That feeling that rested somewhere between hunger and hope.

It was hard to feel anything like hope. His mind kept trying to pull him back to the dark world where his words set off riots and wars. Where his friends were in danger and all he wanted was to be home where his father was sick or maybe still dying. He couldn't do anything about those things now. He couldn't do anything until he solved the riddle of just why he was here. Or anywhere else besides his home. Somehow this feeling he had was the answer. It was wrapped up in Nancy, so one way or another he needed to find her again.

He waited and looked and puzzled on this notion for what seemed like forever. Just when he was ready to make a new plan, there she was, on the corner of the street. Her clothing had changed for a third time. Now she was wearing a black skirt that showed everything inches below her hips. The shoes she wore had long thin platforms that forced her to stand on tiptoes. She was leaning over the passenger side window of a white sedan talking to a nervous-looking man. As she stepped in, Earwig called her name.

"Hey Nancy!" Her eyes locked onto him, narrowing into slits as she got in the car. The man looked away from him but soon turned his car back to the road and then swerved in the opposite direction and they disappeared.

The next day he looked for her at the burger place and under the bridge where the ragged people stayed but she didn't appear in any of those places. So he retreated to a temporary haven, in the patch of woods between those places and that's when she found him.

He didn't know what to make of it at first. Her fingers locked over his right ear and she marched him up the streets to a group of tall red brick buildings and then inside one of those buildings and up a set of stairs.

Chapter 23

Nancy

"How did you know my name," Nancy asked. Earwig stared out the window of her apartment, his right hand still nursing a sore ear. The view was admittedly unimpressive in spite of the fact that everything in this world dwarfed that of his own. All he could see beyond the dusty glass was more red bricks from the neighboring buildings and the black and rusty colored metal grating of the fire escape.

"You won't believe me. I wouldn't believe me, so I know you won't," he answered but her eyes pierced into him and she lifted her chin, waiting so he continued. "In my world and in the other world I traveled to, you were older, much older but you were still you."

He stopped, expecting that this was the point where she would state her incredulity. His eyes darted around the building, looking to see just who she was. Could he trust this Nancy like he trusted the others? Or was her heart twisted here like the heart of his father in the Dark World.

Her desk was piled with medical books. Pictures of her in a cap and gown hung on the wall next to a framed poster with large words that read, *Bachelor Of Science* and smaller words seemed to speak of earning the right to a title and all of the privileges therein. It was a declaration of education. He may have been able to deduce that by all of the books. Books on shelves, books on tables, and books on the countertops.

One of her shelves was decorated like a shrine. It was shrouded in a red cloth with candles with statues and a list printed in bold gold letters that read. *banned and challenged books.* The books on the shelf below had titles on their stems that matched the names of the books on the list. "Gender queer by Mia Kobabe, Lawn boy by Jonathan Evison, To Kill a Mockingbird by Harper Lee. Beloved by Tony Morrison. The Hate You Give by Angi Thomas. Maus by Art Spiegelman, This Book is Gay by Juno Dawson."

Nancy smiled with her eyes as she saw Earwig's attention drawn to her shrine. "Those are the books people tell you not to read. They have ideas that some people don't want you to think about. That makes them the most important books in the world. Never let anyone tie down your thoughts," She said. As if answering the question that he had not yet asked.

The first time he saw her she wore a uniform for BurgerLand and seemed to carry herself in a different light than any of the other times he saw her. She seemed duty bound to that place, much like the slaves in the dark world were duty-bound to their masters. The next time he saw her she was in jeans and a t-shirt, delivering food to the ragged people under the bridge. She seemed to move there with more purpose. The time after that when he called out her name and she looked at him filled with rage and shame, she was dressed in clothing that seemed too slight for the chill in the air. The man in the car she was getting into looked away, hiding a certain level of shame himself.

She was complicated, Earwig decided. It didn't make her either bad or good. Everyone he met seemed to have so many levels of complication.

"Do you still want me to talk or do you just think that I'm crazy?"

"Both," she answered matter of factly. She didn't believe in otherworlds, the supernatural, or anything sci-fi for that matter. She never had and thought she never would. Save for one second when she was in a place she didn't want to be, doing something she didn't want to do. Something that she thought she could think her way out of regretting. Then a kid called her name and when she met his gaze, she knew that she didn't know him and felt like she had known him forever at the same time. Except for that moment and the moment she was in now, it wasn't logical to believe in him. She had no cause to believe in him and yet she did believe him until she thought about it.

Some deeper truth saturated the long story about his homeworld. His trip though the nexus and the dark world, where this other Nancy helped him and the king hide from a dark version of his father and a reincarnated soulless version of the king's son.

He got to the part of the story where the king threw himself in harm's way to push Earwig out of his world and into this one. He explained how he saw her and followed her, trying to determine whether or not she could help him.

After a contemplative pause, she said, "I like that version of me." She said it with a smile but Earwig could see that there was a whole flood of tears behind it that she would never let go of if she could help it. "She's brave, independent and a bit of a badass. She's the sort of woman I wish I could be."

She pulled her degree off of the wall and set it in front of Earwig. "I was the first woman in my family to go to college. I got this here degree. I was well on my way to becoming a doctor of medicine. The thing is, we make our little plans. Then life makes its plans and if the two don't match, life wins.

I took on a few too many loans. I went to a school that cost a little too much. All of the money just sort of dried up. After thousands of dollars and four years of school with a 4.0 GPA, do you know that the only place that would hire me was Burger World because I don't have any practical experience. Which I can't get if nobody hires me and if I don't pay down my loans, I can't get back into school.

Life made its plans but you know what, I made mine. I'm going back to school. I am going to be a doctor. So I found a second job, dancing for lonely men.

I really hate the job but I don't regret it and I'm not ashamed. I was getting a ride there when you saw me. That's the thing though, this other me that you told me about. That doesn't sound like anything she would ever do, so she can't be me."

"She isn't you," Earwig agreed. "I can't imagine my dad ever torturing people or trading slaves. The person I saw in the Dark World may have had his face, name, and body but he wasn't my dad.

My dad always warned me that life would make me choose between doing what's right and doing what's easy. He said I won't always know which is which but I should just try to be as kind as possible. Try to make the world a little better and if I did that things would sort themselves out. He told me this when people were throwing rocks at us.

"Just be kind my boy, they don't hate us. They are just confused," he'd say.

"But they did hate us. They wanted us dead but my dad would just smile, nod, and deliver what gifts he could. Even as people spat on him, swore at him, and threatened to burn down his house. It didn't matter. None of the rocks would hit and their fires went out when they tried to burn down our house but even if they couldn't hurt all of the posturing and words. Somehow the fact that they still did it even though everyone knew it wouldn't work just made it feel so much worse.

My dad could love the whole village through all of that but I couldn't and why should I have to? Why should anyone have to put up with that kind of abuse and still be nice to the jerks who tortured them? That's how I know it wasn't my dad. My dad wasn't the sort of guy who ever wanted much for himself."

It had started to rain while they talked and as the story got longer the rain seemed to pick up into a torrent. Nancy considered her options. Option One: send this strange kid out into the weather to fend for himself. It was the least complicated option. There could be real trouble following him. She didn't want to answer any questions about who he was or why he was at her apartment. It was simple but not right.

Option Two: contact the police, who would contact the county and they would take him off of her hands. This was the option that made the most logical sense. It was the legal way to take care of her problem, but somehow that didn't feel right either. Somehow his story and his damn unnatural blue eyes seemed to cut into her soul.

Option Three: This wasn't an option. (Why the hell was she even giving herself an option three?) The kid was lost. He needed adults to take care of him. Adults who weren't her. He needed psychiatric help and that wasn't her chosen field of expertise.

"You can sleep on the couch tonight," she decided. *"This is stupid,"* she thought. "I'll make us some supper. Egg drop ramen, she said. *"Because I don't have any real damn food."* she thought. "Tomorrow, if you have any idea what you're looking for. I'll try to help you find it," she told him. *"Tomorrow, they'll probably lock me up for abducting an escaped underaged mental patient,"* her thoughts concluded.

Earwig thanked her. In response, Nancy smiled and said, "No problem." This was a problem though, she realized. A real big problem.

The soup she made; ramen with eggs, cheese and her own blend of spices, was an explosion of flavors that Earwig had never tasted before. After dinner and washing the three dishes she owned, Nancy moved on to an exercise routine. She followed that with a video-instructed Wing Chun class where she maneuvered her hands in and out of a wooden pillar with smaller pieces of wood sticking out of it.

From there, she moved on to a video instructing the ballet routine in a mirror. She then doodled in a sketchbook, played with clay, and painted before moving to her smartphone to practice language and math.

Earwig pulled one of the books from her shrine after she offered to let him read anything in the house but he had trouble following along because her nightly routine was almost exhausting to watch. He wondered if back in his home world, his Nancy had a collection of hobbies like this Nancy.

Life had dashed her every plan, but here she was taking on the world. Tasting every bit of life, trying every art. She was a zealot for the love of living.

When asked about her routine, Nancy would be the first to confess that she didn't feel she had any real talent or aptitude in any of her hobbies. She couldn't draw a picture from her mind, couldn't paint the right colors, probably couldn't fight off an attacker, and definitely could not speak fluently in any of the four languages that she was trying to learn. She did what she did, not because she was good at it or because she ever believed she would become good at any of the things. She did what she did because the act of learning, creating, and doing things brought her joy.

The world was a hard scary place and any joy you could bring to it made it just a little less hard and a little less scary and that was all. As she went through the process, Earwig wondered if the fact that she made so much art that nobody would ever see made her more of an artist than the people that went on to be considered great.

On the second day, when she was going through her routine, she offered Earwig several pages of canvas paper. He tried to draw and then paint some of the scenes from his adventure. The lines of the drawing were okay but the watercolor paints he used seemed to wash over the picture, escaping the lines and only landing in the suggested areas.

It's beautiful, she said, looking at his paintings. One was his best effort at painting her but it was her as an old woman. Another painting showed the goat cart on a manure-paved road at home and a picture of the inside of the nexus. He wondered if she was lying to be nice but accepted the compliment all the same. It was nice to hear someone besides his father treat him the way he thought people should be treated.

He was actually proud of one of his paintings. It was an attempted self-portrait that turned out entirely wrong. In the painting, his hair was too long and wavy. His cheekbones were too high. His eyebrows were too thin and his lips too puffy. It looked nothing like him but maybe the fact that he was trying so hard to leave something of himself in it so that when he left this Nancy, she wouldn't forget about him. It made it seem not quite as off as it was. Perhaps he thought the picture captured something in him that he had never seen. He hadn't felt real pride since he was a small child delivering gifts for the first time. Before the reality of how cruel people were had destroyed it.

He thought he would never feel pride like that again. Yet here he was with a far-from-perfect or even good picture and he was as proud. As proud as he had ever felt.

Nancy accepted his painting with a smile, framed it, and hung it on her wall. None of her own pictures hung on her wall but this one did. Earwig felt as though the joy in his heart would make it explode. A part of him, though he was ashamed to admit it, didn't want to go home.

He needed to go to save his dad but maybe afterward, he dreamed. Maybe he could sneak back across the nexus to this place, where he could stay with Nancy. Where he could read books, make art, and feel more accepted and understood than he had ever felt at home.

That wouldn't happen of course because he was heir to the lineage of the nexus keepers and everything he would ever get to be or do was tied to and bogged down by that reality. He would succeed his father, either when his father passed or when he was too old to deliver any more gifts. He would be gifted a kid, which he would have to raise to replace him.

There wouldn't be a ton of time to paint, draw, dance, practice languages, martial arts or sculpt. That time was needed at home to sort out gifts, load up goat carts, roll through town, and try to deliver them to people who hated you.

"Why are you crying," Nancy's voice broke into his train of thought.

"I love my dad, ``Earwig started. I want to find whatever it is I need to find and go back to save him but..," he sighed. "Back home, there is a person that I need to be. A life I need to live. A job that I have to do and it's important. I know it's important but it's not what I want for my life. Don't think I'm horrible but I really don't want to go back. I want the freedom to read, paint, and dance but I know it won't be long after I go back that all of that will be over. I'm also afraid that I don't know what's right anymore.

Everything I tried to do to help people just made things worse. Everyone I tried to save is in danger. The king in the dark world is a good man. The king in my world, I guess used to be good. At least for a while but I'm told only one of them will pass the test.

I'm supposed to let a good man be tortured, broken, and become something he doesn't want. All so that I can save my world from enduring the same fate. Why does one king have to fail so the other can pass? It's not right. If there really is good in both of them, why shouldn't they both be able to keep their hearts?"

Nancy's hand clasped around his. "That's what your grandma said? Mine told my mom that when a white person wanted her seat on the bus, she had to get up and move. Don't make no waves. Don't pick no fights, just move out of those white people's way, but here's the thing. My grandma was trying to protect my mom from what might go wrong but just because she was trying to protect her, that didn't make her right.

" My grandma is a bit of an ancient god though."

:   "All the more reason not to trust her," Nancy interjected. I've seen too much pain and suffering. Your story has too much suffering in it for me to ever believe in infallible gods.

Somewhere along the lines, I suspect the wheels fell off the cart and pretty badly at that. We might not be able to fix everything but if we use our heads and our hearts maybe we can fix the things that are in front of us and the things we can. You just do what you think is right.

Earwig could almost hear his father's voice in Nancy's. "When you don't know what's right, just do your best."

Monday through Thursday Nancy only packed two uniforms into her duffel bag before heading out to work. They were the uniforms that she wore to cook at Burger World and to feed the ragged people under the bridge.

On Friday, she packed what she called her club clothes: short skirts, crop tops, and fishnet stockings. She always said it with a bit of disdain and Earwig could tell something about her job dancing for lonely men, upset her. It was the sort of injury he could tell she preferred to keep to herself. He had gained a few of those, so he didn't want to press it but the look in her eyes made him feel squeamish. Something was wrong.

Over the course of weeks, they had established a routine. She had even picked him up new clothes to replace the war-torn rags he had on and after much hesitation, he learned that the spider silk cloak was washing machine safe. It was a Thursday, one of the last afternoons he would get to spend with her before her work kept her out all night and he would occupy himself with trying to find whatever it was he was looking for. That's when he met Jasmine.

The introduction was startling as Jasmine only knocked half a knock before throwing the door open and saying, "Hey listen, I'm just going to borrow…"

Earwig was confused. It was almost like his picture. Jasmine was tall with broad shoulders. Jasmine's hair was long and wavy. Jasmine wore makeup and a dress. In spite of that, something about Jasmine's voice, (though disguised) throat, and general appearance looked to be that of a man.

"Who the hell are you?" Jasmine asked.

Nancy cut in. "Relax girl! This is my cousin from out of town. Earwig, this is Jasmine. She's a good friend from the club."

"The club," Jasmine said in a sort of *I get it* voice. "Do you really think he's old enough to be knowing about the club? Besides that, what the hell kind of name is Earwig?"

It's actually Earwigregalus Yohonamonstavitchnic. "I'm a… not from Wisconsin."

"You don't say," Jasmine smiled. "Well, a friend of Nancy's is a friend of mine. Promise me you won't grow up to be the sort of guy who goes to the club." Almost the second she finished the thought, her pitch changed and her voice rose, "Oh my gosh did you do this," she gleamed, pointing at his picture on the wall. She looked at him a little bit differently. New approval glowed in her eyes as she nodded. "Anyway, I was hoping to borrow those stockings, you know the ones."

"Tonight," Nancy asked. She had a look of disapproval in her eyes. We promised each other that this wasn't going to be our lives. I'm going to be a doctor. You're going to be a dancer, A legit prima-ballerina."

"There's money out there tonight hun," Jasmine answered. Thursday's the new Friday. The sooner I can get what I need. The sooner I can get on with my life. Don't you start judging me now!"

"Just promise me, you'll stay safe," Nancy said while handing Jasmine the stockings from her club uniforms." Jasmine blew a kiss to both of them falling into an exaggerated bow. "Until next time," she said, closing the door behind her.

Earwig liked her, even though their acquaintance had lasted mere minutes. Jasmine seemed like the sort of person who brought light into every room she entered.

That was Thursday and had he known that things were about to change yet again, Earwig would have done his best to lock every single second into his memories so that none of it could slip away.

Chapter 24

Loss and Escape

Friday morning, Nancy left for Burger World. From what he could find out after the fact, she concluded her shift without incident. She delivered her food to the men under the bridge. After interviewing them, the police determined that they had nothing to do with what happened.

It was late Friday night, or perhaps early Saturday morning before he started to suspect something was wrong. She was always back before three am in the morning. Most club nights, she returned right at two-thirty and took a long shower. Sometimes, when she was showering, he heard her cry.

Afterward, she would pat his head as he pretended to sleep and retired to her room. He never knew what it was but the weekends were hard on her. It was more than the long hours. It was something that stole the sparkle from her eyes.

She never returned and around noon, as Earwig waited, terrified about all of the things that could have happened, he heard two men talking outside of the door followed by the lock being unlocked.

She wasn't there though. There were two police officers. One was a short bald man in a blue uniform. He had seen him once before and Nancy explained that Earwig was just visiting from out of town. There was a look in the man's eyes that Earwig understood. Something bad.

Kid you're gonna have to call your parents, something happened. Your cousin she…"

His head dropped. "Did something happen at the club?"

"The club… Is that what she told you? Aw hell, kid."

Earwig grabbed his cloak and a slice of pizza from the fridge. "I'll just go," he said, knowing what came next and how much choice he would have in the matter. The police took him to the station where they asked him questions about Nancy. He told them everything he could. After that, they asked for a phone number. When he couldn't provide one, they took his picture and his prints. He found out that in this world he was a runaway foster child named Earl. They didn't want him back.

A couple of hours later a man with a suit escorted him to a car. It was a little like the police car but this time they didn't put him in cuffs. They brought him to a large brick building with a sign that read, *Madison Area Juvenile Crisis Shelter.*

"This is temporary kid," a man explained as they walked into the door.

There were more questions, followed by a tour. The tour was punctuated with rules. Lights out at 8:30 p.m. Everyone is up by 6:00 a.m. If you are not in the mess hall by 6:15 a.m. then you don't get any breakfast. You need to sign up to use the rec room. You need to sign out any games you play. TV time is controlled by a list. He tuned out the rules as best he could.

The only room he was really concerned with was the laundry room. There was a spider in the window. A black widow spider. Looking at it, he could tell that the spider was as out of place as him. Its web glowed blue.

That was his way out, but not today. Today they would be watching him. They would recite rules in his ear and do everything they could to make sure that he was going to fall into place. That was what he was going to do for now. Earwig planned to be so polite, quiet, and amenable to whatever it was that they wanted, that he would disappear.

He made it to his meals. He took his shower and washed the clothing that they gave him and the clothing that he came in with, as scheduled every other day. He never asked for the TV or the rec room. He didn't interact with any of the other boys. Instead, he read every book he could find. Everything from medical books to how-to books and science fiction.

The few times someone did interact with him he tried to be polite, even sheepish so that he wouldn't give anything away.

It was always the same questions, an introduction where they traded names followed by the kid interviewing him saying something along the lines of "Whatcha in for?"

He didn't know how to answer that but usually stuck with, "bad luck."

Often they would respond in the same way. Either by saying, "ain't we all" or "you and me both." Earwigregallus smiled and then turned back to his book at that point and the kid trying to interview him, saw the sadness through the smile and at that point dropped the attempt at conversation.

His escape was anything but bold or harrowing. It was his laundry day and having made it a point to be the most boring individual in the room, Earwig tested the window by the spider. As he suspected it was unlocked. He stood on the machine, relocating the spider so he wouldn't smash it.

That's when one of the kids that had interviewed him rounded the corner. His name was Kurt. His question was, how did they nab you?" His generic response was, "you and me both." He paused wide-eyed looking at the boy half out the window.

Earwig locked eyes with him and he could feel the tears starting to flow but he mouthed the word, "please."

Kurt smiled, nodded, and closed the laundry room door. There were no cops, no dogs and until they did a head count and found him missing, nobody really cared.

Just like that Earwig was free but couldn't go back to Nancy's. He wanted to so badly that his soul hurt but he knew that part of his life was over. He went to the only other place he knew that he would be welcomed. He went to disappear, underneath the bridge with the ragged people.

His presence was marked with a shrug and a, "Damn. Sorry kid." That came from one of the men who had seen him and Nancy together and that was all. There were no introductions, no monsters to fight, and no slaves to free. No great ambitions to propel them forward on some noble quest. It was just a group of people surviving the only way they could.

These men, though tolerant of his presence, neither wanted to share any part of their lives with him nor hear about any part of his. Under the bridge, there was a different sort of treachery than that of the dark kingdom. It was more subtle, but in many ways, it was way worse.

During the day, you looked for food. Some of the men got a hold of markers and made big signs out of cardboard hoping that sympathetic motorists would pass out a few dollars or some food. Others looked for kitchens and outreach centers. They were strewn all over town and if you timed it right, it was possible to get three squares in but for Earwig, this was a risky proposition.

In spite of their underwhelming effort to keep him contained, the police still had his picture. His options were the dumpsters and the occasional rat or rabbit. Either that or risk recapture. This time they might put him someplace that was really meant to keep people contained.

At night they returned to the bridge. Some of the men passed around bottles. Some of them shared needles and pipes but nobody said anything about it. Just like in the crisis shelter, there was no talking after lights out.

CHAPTER 25

THE KING OF NOTHING

It was perhaps a week into it when the no talking after lights out rule was broken. Earwig was settled in, not too far from the needle crowd. He was there on purpose because if only for a second, he thought he had seen the king disappearing into a tent.

For the first time since Nancy's death, something that resembled hope returned to him. So he was waiting, trying to reconnect to the nexus and engage the mechanical part of his brain. The part that understood things with no logical reason. It seemed as though that feeling was another thing that had passed with Nancy.

Still, he had seen him and maybe even felt just a shiver of the old knowing before it passed. As he sat there, waiting, watching, and hoping, a group of strangers made their way to the camp. There was cruelty in their laughter and murder in the eyes of the one they seemed to be rallying around.

He was older than Earwig by a few years. Perhaps he was even what passed for an adult in this world. His hair was shaved too. He had a denim vest jacket with no sleeves, revealing tattoos with symbols that Earwig could tell were imbued with darkness. In his arms, an aluminum baseball bat had been spray painted with a word he recognized as a slur, in front of the word *killer.*

The man cursed, "Hey, street rat! Didn't I see you running around with some.."

Earwig didn't hear the words that followed because the bat cracked hard against his face. His world was all at once a blur of boots and steel, pain and half-discernable swear words.

Then out of the madness and the din of battle called another voice. It was king Henesy. "Go on, get!" The cracks were stopped with a clang and a scream. Through his blood-soaked eyes, he saw the king disarm the bat wielder with the handle of a mop while slamming a trash can lid against two of the attackers' heads.

Before he knew it, the men who attacked him were on the ground crying and begging for the king to stop. From his hands, almost mechanical and impossibly fast, came the calls of wack-clang, wack-clang. The attackers made it to their feet, only to be knocked down again.

It was impossible to tell what blood was his own and what was the attackers. There was blood on the can lid, blood on the street, blood on the king's tattered clothing, and blood in his vision. It was everywhere.

The attackers tried to scramble around the king but he maneuvered his weapons to find their marks, just as soon as one got up. The king's assaults only relented when they turned and ran the other way.

He didn't drop a bead of sweat. He didn't pant or give any indication that the battle had exhausted him. The king only laughed.

It was definitely King Henesy, but it was not, of course, the same man. Even in the world where he had been disposed of and was on the run from his army (now under the control of his resurrected son), there was a spark there that was absent from this man's eyes.

He was a vacuous, somewhat wild-looking thing. Something that seemed more animal than man at first glance. All the same, that animal just saved Earwig's life.

"I should thank you." Earwig started holding his head.

"Yeah and I should get my crap together and start living right but it's not likely to happen." The wild Henesy laughed.

"You're a king right?" Earwig asked and the wild Henesy laughed even louder.

"In my world, you're the king of my village but then I traveled to the dark world and you were king there too but you had been deposed. They caught us. They were going to kill me but you risked your life so I could get away. But you're you. You are the Henesy just from, wherever we are here. Surely you must be king here too."

The wild king tapped on the chest of his blue jacket, where embroidered words spelled out the name, *Henry*. "Go back to school kid but first give me whatever drugs you're on!

My name is Henry and I ain't the king of nothing unless you count bad choices as a kingdom. I was about to take my medicine but the thugs made a whole lot of racket trying to murder you near my spot. So you can keep your thanks. I'd rather you just took your crazy somewhere else."

"I don't know if I can. I found my thread. It brought me to you, twice."

"Earwig saw him mouth, "Son of a..," followed by an indiscernible grunt. Then he sighed. "Fine. I will help you on your...," Henry paused and then said, "quest," like it was a question. "But first I need to consult with the gods. So if you aren't going anywhere, just wait over by that corner and pretend you don't exist for about half an hour or so."

Henry rolled up his right sleeve and tied a rope around his arm. "Listen, kid, I need you to just move out of my sight for a little bit. I can't do this in front of you but if I don't do it, things are going to get bad for me and pretty darn soon."

Earwig saw the baggy of powder in Henry's shaking hand and the spoon jutting out of his pocket. The same sense that let him figure out how to work televisions and automobiles came back to him, along with another feeling. Henry was holding his death in his hands and he just didn't know it.

"It's poison," he warned him. I don't know what it is but I can tell you, it's what you would call a bad batch."

Henry's face grew stern. "Listen, boy scout, this isn't a fairytale and I ain't no king. You need to get out of here now. I'm not the sort of person a kid like you ought to be consorting with anyhow, got it."

Earwig looked in the mirror. He could see chains and hooks emanating from the baggy. They were sunk deep in the king's skin, pulling tighter and tighter stretching him out. He could see the soul inside of the king, half in, half out, and writhing.

"Look, just look," he said, holding the mirror in front of the king. The mirror is magic, it shows you the truth."

Henry looked, but he didn't see the chains, he only saw himself. Someone who looked twice as old as he was. Someone who felt more pain than anyone understood.

"I don't see crap. There's no damn magic in Wisconsin, he said. Tears were streaming down his face now. "There aren't any kings and there isn't any magic, there's just me. "There's no magic in Wisconsin," he cried again.

Earwig looked again and he saw the twin monsters tugging at the king inside causing him to stagger as the chains from the baggy pulled him in another direction.

"Yer darn right it's poison. I know it's gonna get me one of these days and I'd sell you my soul for a nickel, if I thought you could stop me but you can't. Nobody can. I don't deserve it." The king's eyes kept on darting to the mirror. He couldn't see his soul. He couldn't see the chains. All he could see was his dying body in a dirty uniform from another job that would probably sack him in a week. He was covered in a grease, grime, and filth that had nothing to do with his work. "Get, get out of here damn you," Henry screamed.

Earwig didn't move though, he couldn't. The king was holding his death in his hands and Earwig knew the second he left, the king was going to push that death into his veins.

For the longest time, they just stood there staring at each other. Henry adjusted his eyes down to look at the baggy and then up again at the kid. After several short eternities passed in between the heavy sighing and staring he cursed, yanking the band crudely from his arm and then he cursed again and again and again, saying just about every word Earwig had ever been punished for saying and adding several new terms to his lexicon.

Earwig just stared at him. His eyes seemed to pierce right through Henry's soul, kind of like that stupid mirror or the kid's insistence that he was a king. "Fine," Henry said. You tell me your story 'cause I'm pretty damn sure that I won't get rid of you before you do and then I'll tell you why I'm such a mess."

"Are you sure, Earwig asked. "Because my story starts long before I was born. About a thousand years in fact."

"Of course, it does." Henry relented and with that Earwig started with everything he could remember from the lineage of his home world. He told Henry all about Sam's act of compassion summoning the Kindness, about King Henesy, the loss of his wife, about his son's life and death, and how the king turned against the nexus keepers and the monsters. He went onwards, telling him about breaking the nexus and how his father swallowed the poison mushroom but couldn't get any medicine. He talked about his quest and his encounter with the much more amiable king from the dark world and how that king sacrificed himself so that Earwig could survive.

Henry listened, and even though the story he was being told was outrageous, something about it felt real and familiar. Maybe it was just because it helped him pass the time and calm the shakes. Maybe it was because something there had a hint of truth inside of the lie.

When Earwig was done, Henry began. "I had a wife, and yes, she was a Judy. My son was Frank. He didn't live to one hundred, he lived to ten. After he was gone, my wife just sort of disappeared. She was always talking about going back to Colorado. I guess she finally went. She just didn't tell me. Henry paused for the longest time. I got in this car accident back when my son was about six, maybe seven. It was just a stupid fender bender, not even serious but it threw out my back." He sighed again looking down at the pocket where he had stowed the baggy.

The doctor gave me these pills to help with the pain. I don't know how it started but I just started feeling like I needed more and more. Pretty soon I'm out and I don't even feel the pain anymore but nothing feels right without them. I get another prescription and then another before they cut me off. A buddy of mine tells me he knows someone who could get me some more.

Eventually, I trade the pills for something a little cheaper and stronger. One day I sneak off to go take my medicine and our house catches on fire. I thought Frank would be okay entertaining himself for twenty minutes, but by the time I get back the whole damn building is burning up. I tried to run inside but I couldn't take the heat." Henry began to sob.

"He's gone. He's..," the king swallowed hard, his eyes betraying what to him might as well have been a thousand years of injury and loss as he mustered the strength to continue. "Soon, so is Judy. After the funeral, she didn't say a damn thing. She just left. I get it. I know why. I just can't get myself free. I ain't a thousand years old though. I'm only forty-five. Hell, my parents are still alive somewhere. I haven't been able to talk to them. I can't look them straight in the face. So that's it. The story of why I'm such a mess. I wish I had some octopus spiders to blame but, nope."

Henry smacked his hands together for emphasis. "It's all me," he paused again. "Listen, kid, I'm not who you think I am and I can't think of anything good that can come from you hanging around with someone like me. Just leave."

Throughout his story, Earwig kept pulling the mirror from his pocket and looking intently into it, as if studying it.

"What's in your pocket," Earwig asked finally.

"Drugs, I told you," Henry replied.

"Your other pocket. I keep seeing it. In one pocket, you have a gift from the Terror. On the other, a gift from the Kindness. What's in your other pocket?"

Henry's face grew stern again but this time it was also frightened. "What are you, playing at Kid. is this some sort of...?" His hand reached down and pulled up a tattered piece of paper. The shop was empty, he was sure. He unfolded it, his eyes bouncing over the bold print. He hadn't even been thinking seriously about quitting. It was just his imagination, the lady's voice saying *"take it."* She just sounded so nice and kind. He imagined that she loved him, even though he knew that nobody did. Not anymore, not after he left his son to die.
"

The king told himself that he had read the advertisement and invented the voice but then here came this kid with a crazy story about two monsters gifting people. One giving people what they need, even when they don't want it. The other gives people exactly what they want, as long as it is also exactly what they don't need. His eyes locked onto the bold print. Hope exists. Recovery is possible. The clinic it spoke of was only three blocks away.

"This is stupid. This is so.., " he started, but the boy's eyes seemed to glow intensely across every sky they encountered, and in the void of Henry's heart, the effect was doubled.

"Fine!" His other hand plunged into his pocket, pulling the contents out quickly and thrusting them into the air. They landed in the gutter, and rolled down the slope into the storm drain. "Walk with me, kid. At least to the door. You walk away now, I promise you. I'll be diving into that drain." Somehow even before Henry said it, he knew that there wouldn't be another choice. The kid had a way of saying nothing and staring at him that spoke volumes.

Together they walked. Neither of them said a word until the address on the card was on a window that split their paths.

"Who the hell are you?" Henry asked, hardly able to believe that anything could compel him to press open the door.

"I think that's what I'm looking for."

"If it means anything kid, you gave me hope. It might be a stupid hope but I ain't never had a smart hope before, so I'll take it." With those words, Henry was gone, off to someplace that Earwig knew he couldn't follow. His dad used to tell him when people rejected gifts, *"you can get people to a door but stepping through it is up to them."* Henry had already stepped through it.

Chapter 26

The Revolution Part 2

He could feel the change in the air. At this point it didn't matter if he found what he wanted or not, it was time to go. The darkness was calling him back. His promise had to be kept in the dark world or the price would be paid.

It was the mechanical nexus keeper part of his brain that had led him to this sudden realization. Since he and Henry parted ways he had been wandering and without thinking about it, he had somehow found his way back to the tree with its portal, a direct path to the dark nexus.

It seemed like a lifetime since he departed his friends and now here it was staring him in the face. For better or worse he was going to know how his final deal panned out.

He expected the worst. Why would the Terror even let him make it back to the dark kingdom, let alone pass through its realm to make the journey? His heart sank with every step across the sandy shores of the moonlit lake toward the glowing black hole of the dead twisted tree. Even before reaching the gate, he knew something was wrong.

The worst thing he could have imagined paled in comparison to the hollow empty abyss he found. The nexus was empty. Somewhere in the distance, he could swear that he heard the faint sounds of metal clanking against metal, shouting, crying, and screaming. There were no taunts from above, below, or off to the sides. No army of spiders or giant tentacles seizing his body.

This was worse, somehow than he had expected. He was alone. The monster had left this space between worlds. It was out there, entirely out there, in the same world as his friends. An unstoppable beast of limitless powers, driven by its insatiable hunger for anger, hate, and chaos. That was when he understood. It was never his plan. The monster had kept its word, somewhat. His friends would be alive for now, until he showed his face. If he didn't they were disposable. If he did…

Earwig pushed those thoughts away. His feet moved faster than his brain, throwing themselves forward until the sounds of the battle went from whispers to roars. Until the smoke stung his throat accompanied by the reek of death.

He threw himself through the hole without stopping to think about it. Falling from a wall, he saw Leroy, Jack, Henesy, Nancy, and a handful of the former slaves that were backed into a corner.

Ahead of them, a score of knights marched inward. Every building, even the castle was ablaze. Bodies in crumpled heaps filled the sidewalks, the windows, and the fountains.

"You shouldn't have come," Henesy shouted. "Leave Now! I know you found what you were looking for. Go home!"

So grandma had kept in touch with his friends. She still fed in this world, in spite of all of this.

"Go to your father, this war is lost," Henesy tried to warn him.

"Yesss," the monster's voice split the sky like thunder. "Go to your father but first, bear witness."

Something boomed and Leroy screamed. He was ten feet off of the ground with a giant spider's leg protruding from his back.

Henesy swung his sword, making the leg and Leroy drop all at once. It seemed as though he was dead, but Leroy stood his face blank. His eyes were white.

"Everyone that you love," the monster's voice shot from Leroy's mouth. "Everything you fought to protect. All of it. Dies here." Leroy's giant hands locked around Nancy's throat. She tried to scream but only managed a faint gargle. Her body fell limp. The tail of a giant scorpion fell from the sky punching into Jack's chest. Within seconds his face turned a sickly black and the skin poured off of his bones.

With one more triumphant bellow, the entire city crumbled around them. For as far as the eye could see, smoldering heaps of brick twisted steel, and dead bodies filled the horizon. Even the guards who fought alongside the monster died. Besides Earwig and the king, the only man left standing was

Philip. It was then that the monster, with its tentacles and legs that extended to the skies and beyond all of the horizon, somehow slithered its way into that body that once held Henesy's son.

"This is your test, King. Kill me, kill me with love in your heart if you can."

Henesy looked at Earwig. His face twisted in grief and fear, even as he tried to compose himself to be the king he needed to be for the only other citizen left in his kingdom.

"I don't know how this fight will end," he confessed. But I know this, my friend, if the end has anything other than despair and madness, that is thanks to you. Now, forgive me but you can't stay."

The king called out an order to the Kindness and a blue tentacle shot up through the rubble, latching onto Earwig and pulling him out of the dark world and into the glowing blue webs of his grandmother's Nexus.

Earwig wanted to run to his kingdom, to his doublewide to find his father and tell him everything. But he couldn't, he could barely stand or breathe. He had been walking again for so long, every step carrying a hidden burden that just got heavier and heavier and now, the weight of all he had endured was crushing him. Tears poured from his eyes like hot rain. A bubble crawled from his heart to his throat, to his head, threatening to explode and kill him.

It had happened too fast, he was too late and there was nothing he could do to change any of it. Earwig buried his face against the soft silken floor and bellowed. Everyone was dead, everything was lost.

Chapter 27

Going Home

"Stand," his grandmother called. It was an order, but it was soft and he could feel the love inside of it.

"I can't. I can't breathe. I can't think. Everything hurts. Everything I do." More tears, more pain. The bubble eased just a little as he tried to vocalize it but what could he say to express the depth of madness or the self-loathing that came with knowing he played a part in the end of everything? Whether or not he had any options didn't matter.

"That Henesy has found the love to protect you," grandmother's voice called. He found that love because of you. For better or worse, he has passed the test."

Her words didn't fix anything. His friends were still dead. It still happened when they were executing a plan that he had made. A deal that he had been willing to make with a creature made from darkness. Yet somehow, even though everything was still broken, that almost minuscule fragment of hope allowed him to pull himself back to his feet.

"Your world needs you now, more than it needs me. I have had… errors in my judgment. Please. Go home," grandmother implored.

He nodded his head and picking up his almost immovably heavy feet, hoisted all of his burdens upon his back once again. He shuffled forward, walking for some hours in silence before stopping again.

"I never thanked you," Earwig said. "You were there. You were always there. In every world, even in the dark nexus, weren't you?"

"Yes," grandmother answered, " I am so much bigger than you see. All Eldritch are."

"But you were with me even when I didn't want you to be. When I was ashamed or afraid. You helped me, without me asking, without me knowing. But I blamed you, I got mad at you. I was afraid of what you would think of me but I never thanked you and I should have. I'm sorry about that and… thank you."

"It is, what I am. What I do."

"I think I know my new name, " Earwig told her. He didn't tell her though, as it wasn't time. She wasn't the person who needed to hear it first. He was saving that for someone else.

When the son of the nexus keeper stepped from the blue gate, lightning seemed to split the sky. Those who had seen him arrive noticed something different about the person who came out. This boy was very much a child when he entered the nexus but now, though he was still quite young, the miles and the madness of experience had left their marks on his face and in his eyes.

"Keeper, tell your monster that the king requests its presence," A guard yelled.

The boy shook his head and muttered," you might want to reconsider that."

One of the guards put his hand on the hilt of his sword but this young man looked all the way through him. There was a challenge in those eyes and a hint of being both tried and unimpressed."

"I'm going to see my father," said the nexus keeper's son. "Just so we're clear, I'm not asking for permission."

Somewhere behind his new disposition, the tattered clothing, the bruises, scars, and the muscles that now existed where once there was baby fat, the air seemed to move in a different way. The guards stepped aside. So he crossed through their formations aware but lacking any indications of fear. Several of the guards cursed but did nothing.

His dad was half sitting, half lying on his bed in the doublewide. "My boy," Macrothele beamed as they embraced. "What happened?"

His son paused, staring at the assembling army outside, considering what it meant for this world before beginning. "I've got a few things to tell you…including my new name."

Outside the bedroom window, hundreds of guards became thousands and soon the villagers joined in. They carried large chains with links made out of steel, thicker than his arms. The soldiers had carts upon carts of spears and swords, which they distributed amongst themselves as they stared with anticipation into the blue, preparing for war. All the while, Macrothele's son watched nervously and told his father about everything he had seen and experienced since he first stepped through the Nexus.

Chapter 28

Deals in the Dark

Henesy had been having the same dream almost every night for five hundred years. It wasn't a dream though, it was a memory and a threat all wrapped into one. In this dream, he was walking as he often did past the room with the book. He wanted to make sure the locks were locked and the remaining guard was in place. But instead of locks and guards, he saw holes that cut through reality, glowing black.

"Do you want to win, king?" It was a masculine voice, deep and raspy. "I can give you eternal life and a kingdom that will outlast time itself but you can't do it alone. Let me in. Let me in and we will starve her out before you even raise your blade."

The dream gets interrupted here and he sees himself shouting at the nexus keeper's son.

"Go now, this is not your fight!" All around him, everything that was once his kingdom is a pile of rubble and death, crushed beneath golden tentacles and metallic blue spider legs. "It's a trap. Don't do it!"

Henesy's eyes crashed open and he clutched at his heart trying to catch his trembling breath. The dream somehow felt worse than it ever had before. It was compounded by the fact that he had let that Terror deliver him gifts and the sudden realization that one thousand years ago today, he made another deal.

Chapter 29

Familiar Objects

"No, no, no," Macrothes son's face twisted once more. There was terror in his eyes, genuine terror. "We need to work and fast."

It took a few seconds for Macrothele to get on his feet and make it to the window. "Those the collars from your story," Macrothele asked. Outside the window, guards and civilians alike were now busy distributing and fitting themselves with the same large metal collars.

His son screamed. "He's here! He's here now! There's another nexus. A dark one, like in Wisconsin." Behind the kid's eyes, the memories of all of his friends being executed for his benefit took over. Tears started to flow and his feet seemed to lose their ability to move. He screamed again.

"Son," Macrothel interrupted trying to get him to refocus., "I know it's bad but you've fought this before, you know how."

"I know how…" the young man replied, scanning the trailer. His heart sounded off like a drumroll. "I've fought this before." He closed his eyes and took a breath. Soon the Nexus Keeper part of his brain, the part that understood things without thinking, took over and started taking inventory: He began looking around the doublewide. Big speakers, ten gauge wire, tools, and….a motor. He could see the machine, every nut, every bolt in his mind. There was only one problem. The crowd was still assembling.

The back door squeaked open and closed followed by three sets of footsteps. He grasped his socket wrench like a hammer pushing himself between his father and the hall as the intruders rounded the corner.

Then he saw the boots. The biggest boots any man had ever worn. The socket dropped. "Leroy!" The boy's arms wrapped around the giant wearing his friend's face. Behind him, Nancy and Jack looked stunned.

"Kid, I don't know you," this Leroy pronounced.

"It's okay. It's okay, Leroy. I know you," Earwig answered.

As the kid's head drove into his stomach, Leroy winced. It wasn't just leftover pain from where Jack stabbed him all those months ago. His brain went back to the boy's departure. When he was laying on the ground bleeding. He thought of Nancy rubbing a burning salve onto his wound, even as he threatened to break free of his ropes and tear her head off.

"You may try," she always answered.

Her confidence wasn't just a show. As Macrothele and Leroy got better, eventually she quit tying him up all. She was too busy making medicine and cooking up enough food to feed a small army to be bothered with the ropes and Leroy couldn't force himself to betray her, not even to escape.

The one time he crept out the door as Nancy was sleeping in a chair, she opened her eyes long enough to say. "If you are going, you better bring your salve and remember a jacket."

He understood then that he was free to go at any time he wanted, yet he didn't go. He wanted to continue to believe the kingdom's lies so that things could be the way they were before but he couldn't and they weren't. After reading the truth in the journals and seeing the proof in pictures, he couldn't help but see that the Kindness seemed to glow everywhere that he looked.

In the weeks that followed, Leroy thought he was coming to terms with his past. Now the kid he had met once on the worst day of his life was hugging him like a family member. Leroy realized that he hadn't come to terms with all of his memories. They hurt worse than the stab wound, so he winced.

"It's bad out there. Real bad," Nancy announced, putting the odd situation aside. She slapped two journals on the table. "This is everything our families have discovered over a thousand years. I'm assuming you may be able to help fill us in on the rest," she asked, directing her attention to the young man whose head was still buried in a bewildered Leroy's stomach.

He pulled away awkwardly and turned back to his machine building. "The Terror is also here. It has destroyed the dark world. I was there. You were my friends. I watched you all die. It used me to start a war that killed everyone and it's here now. It's…" One minute he was speaking and the next, his vision went black. He found himself gasping for breath, crumpled down in a heap on the floor bawling as images of rubble and death consumed all of his thoughts.

Leroy's massive hand brushing his cheek snapped him out of it. "You alright, kid?"

"You've done enough son," Macrothele sat by his side. "You know how," he added. "But you're not alone anymore. We're here for you, all of us. I can build too."

He worked on breathing. He had said so much already but there was so much more he needed to say in order for the others to understand. He could feel them all surrounding him trying to convey sympathy for the obvious trauma he was bleeding.

"No," he started, not wanting them to see how broken he still felt.. "It has to be me. I know in my mind and in my heart that it has to be me. There's so much more that I have to say when the time is right but that time isn't now. Just trust me." The young man stood. The shadows of his caretakers that felt suffocating to him just a minute ago thinned out as they stepped back.

Tears were on his father's face. "We trust you, son, of course, we do."

"I was hurt in ways that I don't know if anyone could ever understand but I'm not dead yet. I'm not as broken as you might think. This is still my fight, dad you're right. If you want to help me, I need a collar and we need to get somewhere safe, but I don't think we are in any position to leave."

The crowd outside immediately riled with excitement as a giant tentacle shot from the Nexus, latching onto one of the collars and pulling it up and away. Another arm shot up from the ground, twisting around the doublewide. The Truth Keepers and Nexus Keepers all stumbled and fell as the momentum beneath them shifted. Seconds later the view outside of their window was of glowing blue silken tunnels.

Nancy, Leroy, and Frank looked out the windows in wonder. He felt that burden lift a bit again, a little relief. His loved ones were safe for the moment. This place didn't fix the horrors that had been tattooed on his brain, but it at least made them feel a little more bearable. Macrothele, on the other hand, felt better than he had in twenty years.

CHAPTER 30

HENESY AND THE KING

Henesy didn't quite understand what was going on. After some hours of being matched blow for blow, he managed to defeat the corpse of his son but the monster inside billowed into the darkness, leaving him injured and sweating in the ruins that used to be his world. Just as he feared, several hours of searching confirmed that everyone was gone.

He was neither a Terror, or a Kindness, nor had he been granted the mercy of death. He was just there alone. King of the rubble. There was nothing he could do for this world. It was lost but he knew where the monster was headed. So into the Dark Nexus, he followed. A fool, on a fool's errand but perhaps it was the only thing there was to do. After all, the monster still lived.

There were no taunts, no attacks, no attempts at even recognizing him. Henesy could feel the darkness radiating from all around him. It was still

185

here, which was good but it had no interest in him anymore. It could kill him any second it chose, that wouldn't require any effort but then again it would be doing him a favor.

He didn't have the nexus keeper's instincts to guide him, just hope, hope, and a distant ever so faint twinkle of blue against the black. The Kindness would get him where he needed to go if she could. He trusted that much but he didn't know where or what it was he needed to face. Onward he marched, all the while knowing and maybe even hoping that the Terror whose interests were not aligned with his, might cut his voyage short.

It didn't. The only hints that the beast even knew he was there were bits of rubble and chunks of people caught up in its webbing. He grabbed a piece of rock as a reminder for when he got to the source of the twinkle. A hole led into a stone building that looked almost like a room he remembered in his very own castle. It was his room but in another world. He was here, but where was this other king?

On the other side of the wall, this world's Henesey watched something scratching its way out of the darkness. It was dressed like a beggar but wearing his face and armed with a fist-sized stone. He rounded the corner before it was all the way out but the thing moved at a marching pace as soon as it spotted him.

It bellowed out, "Henesy," with a voice that was stolen from his own throat. This king drew his sword and turned to face his attacker square.

The dark world Henesy looked at his doppelganger. He had a soft almost pampered countenance to him. It was in juxtaposition with the deep lines caused by his thousand years of grief and worry. He dropped to his knees and tossed the stone forward so it rolled to the other Henesy's feet.

"I was king in a place much like your own, only a lot bigger," he spoke. "On my side, we got the Terror. On your side, the Kindness. This is what that thing made of my world. This is all that's left. Everything is gone! Everyone is dead," the dark king sighed. "I don't understand. You had a Kindness and you let that other *THING into* your kingdom. You're a damn fool, Henesy!"

They locked eyes, the dark world king searching the vacuous gaze of his copy for some sign of hope or for some shred of the man that used to be. A Henesy that could remember love, laughter, and hope. Meanwhile, the Henesy from this kingdom searched the dark world king to see what sort of trick he was playing or trap he was setting. They were both disappointed.

"I remember when I found that book. I hid it because it scared me." the other king spoke. I was tempted into the test, as I imagine you were. We are opposite ends of the same thread. But I eventually looked at that book. I studied it so I could know what I was up against. Did you?"

This Henesy shook his head.

"Let me guess, the Terror promised to help you win. Or to spare the entire kingdom from death, after you kill its sister?" The dark world king scoffed. "That beast doesn't make square deals. Even if you do somehow escape death it won't matter. Whatever it has in store for you or for your kingdom will be far worse. It's farming you Henesy. It's using you to grow fear, hatred, indifference, and suffering because that's what it eats, but every time it feasts, it only creates more of the same to go around."

"When I am done. No monster will dare meddle in the affairs of men ever again." this world's Henesy spat.

"You don't get it. You don't make plans with this thing. You only ever execute its plan. You only think it's your own until everything goes sideways!" The dark king shouted. "Our kingdom, Henesy. Look at it. Get used to it because that's exactly where you are headed."

The dark king turned to leave, hoping to find the boy, to assist in whatever way he could but before he could take another step forward Henesy's blade shot through his back. He had seconds to come to terms with a thousand years, with who he was, and what he had done.

"I forgive you." He said to his other self.

This Henesy bent forward, his face in a defiant rage he shouted, "WHAT?!"

With his last breath, the dark world Henesy pleaded. "You did what you thought you had to. Please...remember Judith, Remember Philip and Pokie...before it's too late."

There it was, the thing that the king had been searching for but was unable to find. It was just a glimmer, only for a second but it was there nonetheless. It was regret. So he could still feel love. There was still hope after all.

As if triggered by his realization, another voice filled the room. One that both Henesy's had come to know, all too well.

"Ohh, she's tricky, isn't she? Do not let her little puppet show distract you. She is vulnerable. Your time is at hand. After tonight there will never have to be another father who buries his son or a husband who buries his wife. We will make this happen. Life ever after, freed from the shackles of death. You know what you have to do."

This was a war, he thought to himself. Nothing was ever easy about war. Every choice has a cost and a consequence. No matter what, there are always casualties. The question that he needed to answer was whether what he was trying to achieve was worth everything he had to do to get there.

They tell you that death gives our short lives a sense of purpose but was it true? Maybe. He wouldn't rule it out. However, it was just as likely that it was the sort of crap they threw at you to mask the pain of understanding how our lives are just a series of losing everyone we care about until, by mercy or menace, we lose ourselves as well. He could end that though. He could make it so that nobody would ever die again. Who knows what purpose life could be filled with if instead of just being gifted a thousand years that passed in a blink, people instead outlived the stars in the sky.

The dead man with his face did have one thing right. The Terror wasn't his friend, it would betray him for its own purpose the second that became possible. It would have to be dealt with and soon before it mucked up everything.

Chapter 31

About Eldritch

The hole stood two feet in front of the wall, impossible in its depth. The inside of this hole seemed to be shining darkness. It was also thin. The king could walk past this hole and the moment he did, it disappeared. From behind the hole, it wasn't there at all. From the other side, there was only a two-inch by two-inch triangle of black deep emptiness floating mid-air. He could not see the front of the hole again until he was almost directly in front of it. As he walked more degrees to complete the circle, the triangle grew, changing into a diamond, an octagon, then a star with thousands of points before finally becoming the hole.

His brain could only process three-dimensional objects but this fourth-dimensional object with three-dimensional edges forced it to do all sorts of gymnastics as it attempted to try to make sense of something it just wouldn't grasp.

.

What the remaining Henesy was truly concerned with now, was not the dark nexus itself. Behind the hole, on the side where it disappeared, stood a door that he had locked over a thousand years ago. The one he had worn the key for around his neck all that time. Even when there were five guards with orders to keep him away from that door at any cost. Now there were none. He'd sent them all to the Nexus.

Inside the door was a series of locked vaults leading to a chest that contained a single book. The most evil book to ever be put to ink. The title of the book was, **Summoning, Serving and Surviving Eldritch Monsters for Dummies. A Complete Idiot's Guide.**

The king swallowed hard. All the vaults were unlocked and the chest lay open. His trembling hands pulled the book from the last of the boxes and he read:

INTRODUCTION:

So you have discovered a *nexus*. If there is any good news to be contained in these pages it is that those who seek to actively summon an Eldritch will likely be met only with disappointment. One would find it easier to summon a mountain top to their feet than to subjugate these majestic beings. They have existed since a time before time, before the universe's themselves when the aether of existence was but a void.

While seldom credited, it is theorized that the creation of the universes was a direct result of a game being played by the

Eldritch at the time. One which is perhaps still being played to this day. Not that it would matter to you. If you are reading this guide, it is very likely the result of you finding a nexus and wondering; *Just what in the blazes is that thing?*

In the best-case scenario, you happened upon this book after discovering what appears to be a hole in your reality that defies logic.

In the worst-case scenario, you were gifted this book.

So just what in the blazes is that strange hole in reality? Let us begin by giving you a quick lesson in Geometry. In most universes, life is constrained by three spatial dimensions and one temporal dimension. You can move up or down, forward or backward, and from side to side. You experience time from beginning to end. This is not true with the Eldritch.

For starters, though they may visit your universe from time to time, they do not solely exist within it. Rather they make their home in the *Aether*, the space between universes. Eldritch often make a nest for themselves, linking different temporal positions in different universes distinguished by an aspect of choice.

If this concept is hard to understand, then think of it like this. When you look at yourself in the mirror and hold up your right hand to touch the mirror, your reflection will hold up its left hand to match you. The analogy is perhaps a bit crude, for if you were to follow the arrow of time backward in these universes to the point where that mirror reflection held up its right hand and you held up your left hand, you could in theory, reach a place where the choice was being made. Where there was only one world; however, if you continue to go back from that point you would find, again, that everything separates.

The Eldritch experiences time much differently than you. The full extent of which is still not quite understood. While not strictly constrained by the arrow of time like us, they do not always seem to be aware of how every choice will turn out. They experience time as threads being pulled. Much like they experience space with dimensions that we cannot yet imagine, other than mathematically.

So a nexus is in essence, a nest weaved together with threads of potentiality in an extradimensional space connecting temporal positions in parallel universes. It really is that simple.

This brings us to the question that you should have been asking all along. What aspect of Eldritch are you dealing with? Now for the bad news or good news. Even if you were fortunate enough to be blessed by a Kindness, they cannot exist in the absence of a Terror. Just as light cannot exist without darkness to be illuminated. Darkness is meaningless in a void that has never known light. These two beings come in unhappily bonded pairs.

What does that mean for you?

If your town, village, or kingdom is receiving gifts from a Kindness: meant to ease its burdens and amplify its capacity for compassion, love, and hope.

Your twin world and twin self is receiving gifts from a Terror: meant to inspire selfishness, jealousy, division, and hatred.

Don't make the assumption that just because one monster has chosen to feed in your world, the other will leave you alone.

In fact, the presence and promotion of one aspect often amplifies the existence of the opposite aspect.

An abundance of love often makes anger, resentment, and hatred deeper.

An abundance of suffering is often fertile ground for hope,

Hence the Eldlrich are so immense in stature. It is believed that aspects of them permeate every particle in the universe. It is in this way that they are always feeding and always growing.

They are storing the aspects that they are feeding upon in the webbing of their nexus, to fuel them and give them power for the long eternities between the birth of universes.

So you've discovered a nexus. What's next?

If it is not too late, the best advice I can give you is to run. Be it for one year or a million, these things almost always end badly for everyone involved.

But what if it is too late?

What if you were given this book by an Eldritch?

What if you were foolish enough to drink a drop of its blood?

In that case, you may be tempted to fall into despair. However, even then hope remains. For if you were offered and accepted the gift of the creature's blood, then the creature is nearing the phase of its life known as *Fruiting Body Decomposition...*

Henesy read from cover to cover. This time the book didn't feel evil. It felt like a weapon and in the corners of his mind, a plan began to form.

"Monster," he called into the void. "It is time. I need you. Pull the other monster from the Nexus, Pull her all the way out or as much as you can so that my guards can tie her down. Can you do that for me," the king asked?

"It shall be done," the Terror spoke.

The king's hand dove into his pocket and pulled out a small walkie-talkie. He pressed a button with his thumb and announced. "There is a second monster, one clad in gold. Stand at attention and let him pass out of the Nexus. If he brings forth our monster, chain it down."

CHAPTER 32

BATTLE OF THE BEASTS

The commotion of tiny ant-like shadows he had been watching from the windows of his castle grew still as a shadow passed over the sky. The king hadn't expected that. He had assumed that it would crawl from its nexus to hers. After all, they were connected. Instead, it appeared from some impossible height in the sky and slithered down over the entire kingdom. Even the Kindness, so large that she was impossible to know, was dwarfed when compared to the Terror he had unleashed. Henesy swallowed, afraid that it knew what he was up to. It knew he was planning on betraying it and even how and was preparing its revenge.

He pushed the thought aside and watched. He couldn't afford to think like that. He couldn't afford to feed it because the more he fed it, the more it would know him. So he watched. He watched as the sky went black with its unknowably large assemblage of tentacles, legs, and spikes. He watched until the sky cleared again as it crawled and somehow oozed itself into the Nexus and when he was certain that the beasts were occupied with each other he acted.

Back in the doublewide, Macrothele called his son and companions attention to the window again. Grandmother's legs were dancing frantically overtop of them, twisting fine threads into an invisible cocoon around them. Her tentacles flashed around them and all of a sudden, they were back outside of the Nexus. The collared soldiers and villagers around them stood at almost perfect attention but one small group of guards who had yet to receive their collars turned to look and attempted to approach, sensing something was off.

It was almost comical. One of the six guards walked toward the unseen edge of the cocoon but found himself hundreds of feet away and facing away from the trailer. Another one approached from a different angle but fell on his face from five feet in the air. A third tried again. He was more hesitant and cautious than the others but it didn't matter. This guard found himself thousands of feet from where he started. The last three guards decided it wasn't worth the trouble and just turned around and walked away.

Then the sky darkened and everyone without a collar started to run. They would stop their dashes and fall to the ground, screaming, weeping, and lashing at the air as the beast passed overhead. It was like Grandmother, except adorned in gold. Everywhere its shadow touched, those that weren't already collared lost every bit of courage, constitution, and sanity they had. It was followed by a web of putrid black threads that set the forest to rot and buildings to crumble and burn. Its brief passage through their world decimated the village in seconds.

Fortunately for the people, it hadn't given them the same attention it gave to the people from its realm. Instead, it simply entered their Nexus. Seconds later, the two Eldritch had begun to latch onto one another both pulling the other back into their world. Even the skies shook as the terrible struggle ensued.

Both monsters intertwined, lashed, snarled, and bit. More buildings fell, shaken apart by the rumbling of their massive bodies crashing around. Worse than any earthquake. Needles and leaves bounced off the very trees. Sandstone bluffs and mountains crumbled.

Macrothele embraced his son, who was crying and fighting to make it to the door. "What's the point, dad?" What's the point of all of this if that thing is here now? What's the point, if it's just going to kill her!"

"There's nothing we could do to stop what's going to happen, one way or another, but she wanted us safe," he answered.

Nancy took the young man's trembling hands. " I think your job now is the same as ours have always been, to seek out and know the truth. It's ok."

But it wasn't ok. The grandmother that he had denied for so many years was suffering. She was screaming out in anguish as she resisted the assault of the Terror and now after all of this time, he understood just how deeply he really loved her and how much he stood to lose. "Grandma," he cried! He was reaching out for something he couldn't see but he could feel it in the pit of his stomach, in his heart and throat all at once.

Then another sound came, not grandmother but the Terror itself shrieking out in pain, fear, and anguish. Its unearthly bulk sounded somehow small and meek.

Back at the castle, miles away, King Henesy executed his plan. His answer wasn't only in the words of the book but also in an illustration of a castle covered in webbing, the same way his had once been. In the picture, the webbing was ablaze. It made him remember. It was flammable! According to the book, the webs were also where the beast stored their power. Once he was sure that the Terror was fully engaged and once he was sure that it hadn't read his mind, he simply threw a well-oiled lantern into the Dark Nexus and ran to his carriage.

As the carriage charged towards the other nexus, the booming of thunder seemed to split the sky. It was followed by a heat burst from behind as the castle disappeared into a heap of smoking rubble. In front of him, as he approached the blue opening, the Terror's sudden bellow of anguish and agony stopped the horses in their tracks.

As the beast howled, he could feel the air pulsating around him. There were piles of broken rocks where mountains had stood only a few minutes before and they bounced up and down, to and fro, with the Terrors' desperate cries.

Unable to ride any closer with the terrified horses, Henesy tore two strips from his shirt, twisting them in his fingers before pressing them deep into his ears as he jumped from the carriage and marched on towards the Nexus. The battle had spilled outside. The Kindness now stood above a shrinking and shrieking Terror pinning it to the ground.

Two voices fought for control in Henesys brain. The first was the terror hissing, "Do it, king! Do what your predecessor could not! Strike me dead!"

The second was the Kindness, "Be careful. This is a trap."

She was right of course because everything the Terror ever did was a trap or part of one but still he felt he had no choice. Henesy knew that if he drove his sword deep into its heart, the beast would be gone, sort of. The book was a little vague on *fruiting body decompositions*.

He marched straight into the exposed belly and drove the blade forward. And then there was only one voice in his head. That of the kindness "You fool Henesy. You gave him exactly what he wanted."

FRUITING BODY DECOMPOSITION:

The Eldritch are eternal and therefore unkillable but just because something cannot die does not mean that it spends eternity without changing. A *fruiting body death* or fruiting body decomposition is actually a fairly common occurrence throughout the Aether. In worlds where mushroom hunting is important, mycologists often observe that one cannot kill a mushroom by simply plucking and eating it. This is because what we think of as the mushroom is only a very small part of the organism. The *mycelium,* which you may liken to the roots of the mushroom, compose the bulk of the organism.

Mycelium can be many times greater than the size of the mushroom, the part which is often plucked and eaten. Like mushrooms, the part of the Eldritch that you see is often just one aspect of them. Their real size (much of which exists outside of our three dimensions) is unknowable but permeates every molecule in existence.

The fruiting bodies of the Eldritch, what is often thought of as the monster, is a manifestation they create in order to interact with lower dimensional beings. This enables them to attain the emotional energy upon which they are dependent for survival.

So while the real monsters are eternal, their three-dimensional manifestations are in fact very temporary and must be culled from time to time in order for the beings to expand and grow. This process is a combination of molting, like an insect shedding its exoskeleton, and sporing like a fungus sending seeds of itself out into the wind.

Clouds of black billowed from the enormous golden corpse forming a thick fog that enveloped the king, his kingdom, and perhaps even the world. Henesy just stood, sword in hand staring deep into the eyes of the Kindness.

"It's been a hell of a ride, beast. Some of it wasn't half bad but dare I say, for the most part, you drug us through hell," Henesy spat.

"I gave you what you needed most then sat back and let you drag yourself wherever you chose," grandmother answered calmly.

"And now you will submit to whatever I choose," the king asked.

The monster extended one of her massive tentacles, touching it ever so gently against the King's cheeks, before answering. "Yes."

Henesy cursed. His eyes dropped to his feet for the longest time, he struggled to return the monster's gaze,

"You don't deserve what's coming. You really don't and I'm sorry for all of the pain I caused and may soon cause you but..." his eyes returned to his feet.

"Death is the real monster. It's the real Terror. I can end it, for everyone, forever. Except for myself, I won't partake."

He turned sharply away from the monster's gaze to one of his guards. "Prepare the bread!" He turned to a different guard next. "Secure her." He then pivoted on his feet, his eyes somehow avoiding looking directly at the monster or the consequences of his actions as he strode away to a nearby tent.

Chapter 33

The Messy End

Inside the double-wide, it was hard for Macrothele's son to peel his eyes away from the tragedy going on outside for long enough to figure out how to fix his machine to work with the new collars. Every second he wasn't watching felt like an eternity where a thousand terrible outcomes were imminent.

It was only after he finished it that he realized there was something worse than what he had anticipated. Had the machine not worked, it would have been one thing but it did work. The second that he pressed the button thousands of collars clanked to the ground.

Yet nothing changed. The bakers stuck by their bread and the guards continued securing ropes and chains around the monster. Nobody, beyond those in the doublewide, seemed to care at all about the horrific thing they were preparing to do.

Worse yet, they seemed happy. They were eager to greet immortality, even if it meant killing a being of pure love and kindness to achieve that end.

"Why are they.. Why are...Why are they… " he cried. Macrothele tried to comfort him with a hand on his shoulder, but it was no use.

He was broken. Watching the whole damn village eagerly prepare to kill his grandmother, broke his mind, and his heart. He was so angry, so sad, and so confused that he couldn't even string together enough words to complete a thought. They were still there, all of them. Not one person left after being freed.

Outside of the doublewide, the day turned into night. The sweet smell of cherry wood in brick ovens and loaf after loaf of rye bread rose into the air.

The body of the Terror was now no more than puddles of slime on the ground but the memory of his smoke and menace still filled the air. The stars came out, cicadas, crickets, and night larks sang in their evening choir. Children danced and played and the adults gathered, engaged in small talk, all the while full of cheer around the giant monster.

From his tent, the king watched this jolly apocalypse. Something in his heart sank and twisted. The work he had done for all of those years, he feared that he had done a little too well. He was going to do what he had to do but he hated the thought of the whole damn kingdom celebrating the execution of a beautiful soul.

Once, a long long time ago the festivities that surrounded public execution didn't bother him. Back then it was the way of the world. The way it was when he grew up and the way that he thought it would always be but it really wasn't that way anymore.

Nobody had been executed in a thousand years, so why would his people be so eager for this one. Why was he so... not.

It didn't matter. It was time. He exited his tent sword and hand and approached the beast. His eyes turned down with every step, looking up just enough to see where she raised a section of her legs, exposing her beating heart to him.

"Any last words," Henesy asked.

"No," the beast responded.

Inside of the doublewide Macrothes, a broken boy stood. "No," he screamed. Throwing himself to the door. "Noo! Nooo! Nooooo!!"

After everything he had seen and done... After everyone he had lost, this couldn't be the end of the story. He wouldn't let it be.

Behind that broken person his father and the truth keepers followed. They tried to catch him, to stop him from charging head first into his own fate but the boy's feet grew more determined with every step.

When he cleared the cocoon, instead of reappearing somewhere on the inside he landed between the king himself and the monster. Tears poured down the young man's eyes as he reached down deep trying to summon the words that needed to be said.

"Grandfather, Stop," he screamed, his voice piercing through the madness, "Stop, It's time to stop!"

"I don't even recognize you." the king shot back… It was a lie though, for when his eyes brushed across those deep intense eyes he could feel the way their threads intertwined and he could see a glimmer of his Philip there..

The boy stepped forward, steadying his breath. " Then let me introduce myself. My name is Hope Yohonamonstavitchnic. I am your great great, great, great… Let's just say, I'm your really great-grandchild. I have traveled through the Nexus to all the worlds that it connects. We were friends on the other side. I get what you are trying to do. I know how much it hurts to lose everyone you love again and again for a thousand years. I know you think that you are going to spare other people that pain but you're wrong. One version of you fought the Terror because the only thing that gave his life purpose after being granted so much time was trying to protect people.

Another version had never seen the monster, but I could see its imprint all over him. He lived under a bridge, where he took poison every day because the sickness from the poison was the only thing that let him cope with his grief. I saw him confront that monster without ever seeing it. You have forgotten who you are. You've forgotten how damn strong you can be

You have forgotten just how damn much you can love. My name is Hope and I found myself and took my name from you. You were the reason I survived and came back home, so please, please stop this madness!"

Henesy, locked eyes with Hope, the nexus keeper's son, and then with the monster.

"I have something to show you," Hope said, pulling out the mirror. "It shows something different to everyone, but it always shows you the truth. The king's free hand reached forward clasping the mirror, but his eyes remained on the impossible child, standing firm between him and the monster.

First, there was the question of how he got there, but since a magical multidimensional being was involved, that question was a little less interesting than just how the hell the kid got to be that brave. After a moment of hesitation and confusion, the king's eyes turned to the mirror and to himself.

The sword fell with a clang and all at once Henesy was crumpled over onto his knees crying like a child. I just miss my... I just miss my family! He exclaimed. His eyes met the monsters and her giant profusion of eyes seemed to be smiling.

"Release her," he ordered but neither his guards nor the citizens moved very much.

They stared back at him in wild disbelief with an expression of contempt he had never before known. Henesy's eyes turned to Hope. "Run, into the Nexus kid. Hurry, " he pleaded.

He was too late. The crowd exploded forward, betrayed and angry. They weren't going to free the beast and they knew from the king's propaganda that they couldn't kill it but they also knew that there was a loophole.

The beast had to be stricken down by the king's hand. It didn't say anything about him having to be a willing participant. They were all over him and Hope. Henesy watched as the ropes were tied to each of Hope's arms and legs and then tied to the saddles of four different horses.

As the horses walked in different directions, Hope lifted off of the ground, his arms and legs played out and his face twisted in anguish.

"Please," the king begged, "please don't!"

A whip cracked but the horses fell where they stood. They were either asleep or dead, he couldn't tell. Then the ropes turned black and slimy, disintegrating off of Hope's hands and legs. Grandmother's last act of defense for him. By now, familiar with the monster's magic, the villagers returned their focus to the king. Hope stood again, trying to break through the crowd but there was nothing he could do and no way to reach the Henesy.

The angry crowd had rushed over to the king, forcing his own sword into his hand. He tried to pull away but there were too many of them and they were far too strong. He could feel the sword make contact with the monster, piercing her skin and plunging deeper and deeper. He could feel the blade throb as it touched the creature's heart and then the crowd pushed his hand harder.

"Please, I'm so sorry." Violent white light flooded the landscape in concert with a long somber drone that rattled in people's teeth and bones. It was followed by silence and nothingness.

Most of the villagers don't remember what came next. They woke up in their own beds in the same old houses that seemed somehow new. They had headaches, earaches and they suffered from terrible nightmares.

One of the common nightmares repeated through several families was of a skeleton in a bathtub full of diamonds, gold, and coins. As the villagers filled their pockets, the skeletons called out, "greedy greedy, greedy." Or they watched in a window as thin-bodied starving children attempted to reach through and grab the jewels, which turned to bread in their hands. But instead of allowing the starving children to eat the villagers pushed them away, filling their pockets and the skeleton mocked, "greedy, greedy, greedy. Greedy, greedy, greedy!"

The starving children died, turning into skeletons themselves but the dreamers kept filling their pockets and all of the skeletons called out in unison, "greedy, greedy, greedy." When they awoke the villagers and guards were awash in shame and guilt but they didn't know why and wouldn't for quite some time.

The king's perspective was different. He was fully immersed in sorrow bellowing out, "No, don't die. Please don't die," as he felt the blade slide in and break through the beast's heart and then... he was in the Nexus. The sword was no longer in his hand. Instead, the book was. This time it was turned to a page that had always been blank before. Now there were words on it.

...and so it is that after relieving itself of the fruiting body that the monster's full potential is realized. They are no longer bound to the physical world and they are returned to what they

truly are; beings that exist everywhere throughout all of time, all at once."

"You could not kill me king, nor could you kill the Terror.," grandmother's voice called out to him. "You could only free us."

" I didn't mean to… I mean, I did initially but I didn't," the king stammered."

The monster's laughter came from all around him. Her body, now limp and strewn about the ground, was releasing a cloud of blue smoke-spores.

"You did well. In fact, you passed the test."

Henesy smiled. It was one of the first true smiles he'd had in centuries. It was the first time in centuries that he felt hope. Hope that he may see his beloved, his son and his dear friend and occasional enemy Sam, once again.

"My family, he asked. I have waited a thousand years."

Behind the king, Hope, Nancy, Macrothele, Leroy, and Jack had found their way to each other and were watching through the Nexus door. It was shrinking and growing, pulsating blue, black, and white.

"They are with me, waiting for you."

Henesy's felt the weight of a thousand years lift from him. His body began releasing twin particles of black and blue, the colors of both kindness and terror. His face twisted evoking confusion and then the monster spoke again. Its voice was now neither male nor female but something in between.

"I told you, I was bigger than you could see. Nothing is ever only one thing but it's okay king, you had a mighty measure of love to go along with the darkness and so did your family."

It was only then that he understood. It may have had two faces and two voices but there was only one monster.

There was another flash of white and it was all gone. The king, the monsters, and the nexus. All that was left was the village, made out of one double wide surrounded by mud huts and streets paved in goat manure.

In the years to come, the villagers would continue fighting off nightmares of their own making. The kingdom's truth keepers told stories that nobody would believe. Not until another nexus opened; many distant lifetimes in the future, when an act of kindness and an act of cruelty were reflected in two different worlds, like opposite hands reflected in the image of a mirror.

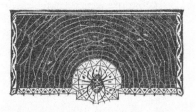

Chapter 34

Minnesota Goodbye

You may have guessed at this point that this story is concluded but this is not the end of the whole story. Yeah, you're sort of correct but I wasn't raised to just say goodbye once. I grew up in Minnesota and if there is one stereotype that rings true about Minnesotans it's that we can't just say goodbye once. Perhaps we're just starving for company or perhaps we have just learned to value our friends so much. Either way, there is a bit of a process which I am now going to walk you through. First, we say goodbye.

So goodbye; however, I just remembered something that wasn't important to me a minute ago and that now I am desperate to express before we part. Often it's a joke or memory we shared, in this case it is a recipe.

Don't worry, I won't end it with the recipe. There are other things to express, other things I forgot. Details that would have seemed tedious when we were talking earlier that I will set in the following pages for you to take or leave. Eventually, I will go, thrilled to have extended our conversation that much longer and I hope that you feel the same way.

I am sad to report that the recipe that Mr. Morris gave to Philip has remained a secret for over a thousand years. What I have discovered of it was that it was a traditional style pumpernickel, baked in a homemade wood-fueled ceramic oven at very low temperatures.

While I was not able to acquire the famous secret recipe, I have discovered something similar on the website www.thefreshloaf.com

I offer this recipe to you now for your consideration should you wish to experience something similar to the flavor that set young Philip's heart ablaze and kept it burning for nearly a century.

Traditional Pumpernickel Rye Bread

1. For the preferment: 50g sourdough starter, 350g cracked rye, 350g water

2. For the Rye Berry Soaker: 200g rye berries, 200g boiling water

3. For the Cracked Rye Soaker: 200g cracked rye, 200g water

4. For the dough: 500g cracked rye, 150g water, 22g salt, 100g maple syrup.

Method:

1. First day:

- prepare the preferment

- put the rye berries in boiling water and cover

- place the cracked rye in water (room temp) and cover

Leave to rest for about 16 hours.

2. Second day:

- place the rye berries in boiling water on the stove and boil until soft (about one hour). Discard any remaining water and leave to cool down.

- Prepare the dough by mixing the preferment, rye berries soaker, cracked rye soaker and remaining dough ingredients and leave to rest for 15 minutes.

- Place the dough in baking tins. Because the loaves will be baked slowly over 14 hours, it is paramount that steam does not escape, as such cover them thoroughly in both baking sheets and foil (I used 5 layers just to make sure, after all I didn't want 3 days of my life to be completely wasted). :) - Bake for 14 hours at 120 C. The classical method states that the temperature should be gradually reduced, but I skipped that part and baked

it at 120 for the entire time.

- After the 14 hrs have elapsed, shut down the oven and leave the tins inside the oven for 1 hour longer.

- Take the loaves out of the tins and leave to rest inside linen couches for at least 24 hours more. Resist the urge to cut through immediately after being removed from the oven at all costs.

The next day, you can finally enjoy the pumpernickel bread.

For as long as we have been able to express our ideas in writing, there have been people who desired control over what ideas other people are allowed to express or consume.

One of the founding ideas in the constitution of the United States of America is the freedom of the press and the freedom of speech. The unencumbered exchange of thoughts and ideas is what allows people to speak truth to power and seek accountability for those who would otherwise seek to oppress us.

This core freedom holds together all of the other freedoms we enjoy. That being said, there has recently been a movement funded by large organizations that aims to censor what books are available to the public, especially to younger readers.

Often these organizations claim to be protecting the reader. However, the ultimate goal is really to make would-be readers incapable of defending their minds from the onslaught of homophobic, racist, and xenophobic belief systems.

The following is a list of books that you may find empowering if you are brave enough to challenge those who would otherwise tie down your mind.

I will not be providing descriptions of the books here or listing why they were banned or challenged. I myself have not read all of the books on this list yet.

Nancy was working towards reading every book on the list when she met Hope. I will admit that she had gotten a lot further than me. If she were still alive she likely would have finished the entire list by now.

All of the books on this list come from the American Library Association which can be located at www.ala.org

NANCY'S SHRINE OF

BANNED AND CHALLENGED BOOKS

The Absolutely True Diary of a Part-Time Indian by Sherman Alexie

Captain Underpants (series) by Dav Pilkey

Thirteen Reasons Why by Jay Asher

Looking for Alaska by John Green

George by Alex Gino

And Tango Makes Three by Justin Richardson and Peter Parnell

Drama by Raina Telgemeier

Fifty Shades of Grey by E. L. James

Internet Girls (series) by Lauren Myracle

The Bluest Eye by Toni Morrison

The Kite Runner by Khaled Hosseini

Hunger Games by Suzanne Collins

I Am Jazz by Jazz Jennings and Jessica Herthel

The Perks of Being a Wallflower by Stephen Chbosky

To Kill a Mockingbird by Harper Lee

Bone (series) by Jeff Smith

The Glass Castle by Jeannette Walls

Two Boys Kissing by David Levithan

A Day in the Life of Marlon Bundo by Jill Twiss

Sex is a Funny Word by Cory Silverberg

Alice McKinley (series) by Phyllis Reynolds Naylor

It's Perfectly Normal by Robie H. Harris

Nineteen Minutes by Jodi Picoult

Scary Stories (series) by Alvin Schwartz

Speak by Laurie Halse Anderson

A Brave New World by Aldous Huxley

Beyond Magenta: Transgender Teens Speak Out by Susan Kuklin

Of Mice and Men by John Steinbeck

The Handmaid's Tale by Margaret Atwood

The Hate U Give by Angie Thomas

Fun Home: A Family Tragicomic by Alison Bechdel

It's a Book by Lane Smith

The Adventures of Huckleberry Finn by Mark Twain

The Things They Carried by Tim O'Brien

What My Mother Doesn't Know by Sonya Sones

A Child Called "It" by Dave Pelzer

Bad Kitty (series) by Nick Bruel

Crank by Ellen Hopkins

Nickel and Dimed by Barbara Ehrenreich

Persepolis by Marjane Satrapi

The Adventures of Super Diaper Baby by Dav Pilkey

This Day in June by Gayle E. Pitman

This One Summer by Mariko Tamaki

A Bad Boy Can Be Good For A Girl by Tanya Lee Stone

Beloved by Toni Morrison

Goosebumps (series) by R.L. Stine

In Our Mothers' House by Patricia Polacco

Lush by Natasha Friend

The Catcher in the Rye by J. D. Salinger

The Color Purple by Alice Walker

The Curious Incident of the Dog in the Night-Time by Mark Haddon

The Holy Bible

This Book is Gay by Juno Dawson

Eleanor & Park by Rainbow Rowell

Extremely Loud & Incredibly Close by Jonathan Safran Foer

Gossip Girl (series) by Cecily von Ziegesar

House of Night (series) by P.C. Cast

My Mom's Having A Baby by Dori Hillestad Butler

Neonomicon by Alan Moore

The Dirty Cowboy by Amy Timberlake

The Giver by Lois Lowry

Anne Frank: Diary of a Young Girl by Anne Frank

Bless Me, Ultima by Rudolfo Anaya

Draw Me a Star by Eric Carle

Dreaming In Cuban by Cristina Garcia

Fade by Lisa McMann

The Family Book by Todd Parr

Feed by M.T. Anderson

Go the Fuck to Sleep by Adam Mansbach

Habibi by Craig Thompson

House of the Spirits by Isabel Allende

Jacob's New Dress by Sarah Hoffman

Lolita by Vladimir Nabokov

Monster by Walter Dean Myers

Nasreen's Secret School by Jeanette Winter

Saga by Brian K. Vaughan

Stuck in the Middle by Ariel Schrag

The Kingdom of Little Wounds by Susann Cokal

1984 by George Orwell

A Clockwork Orange by Anthony Burgess

Almost Perfect by Brian Katcher

Awakening by Kate Chopin

Burned by Ellen Hopkins

Ender's Game by Orson Scott Card

Fallen Angels by Walter Dean Myers

Glass by Ellen Hopkins

Heather Has Two Mommies by Lesle´a Newman

I Know Why the Caged Bird Sings by Maya Angelou

Madeline and the Gypsies by Ludwig Bemelmans

My Princess Boy by Cheryl Kilodavis

Prince and Knight by Daniel Haack

Revolutionary Voices: A Multicultural Queer Youth Anthology by Amy Sonnie

Skippyjon Jones (series) by Judith Schachner

So Far from the Bamboo Grove by Yoko Kawashima Watkins

The Color of Earth (series) by Tong-hwa Kim

The Librarian of Basra by Jeanette Winter

The Walking Dead (series) by Robert Kirkman

Tricks by Ellen Hopkins

Uncle Bobby's Wedding by Sarah S Brannen

Year of Wonders by Geraldine Brooks

Epilogue

Henry

Some of you may still be wondering what became of Henry after he disappeared behind the doors of the clinic. While it is pleasant to think that that was the end of his story, it is unfortunately not true.

Addiction is hell. One cannot expect to go into treatment and be done with it all at once. While time and practice may make it easier for him to stay clean, the temptation to use is something he will have to negotiate for the rest of his life.

He was able to come clean for a time and reconnect with his parents but he always felt like there were invisible teeth chewing at his nerves. His heart pulsated with agitation and one day it was too much to bear. Within two phone calls, he obtained more heroin and the needles to inject it.

While under the influence, he felt separated from the magic of the day he met Hope. Henry attempted several times to take his own life. He cut his wrist with broken glass. He ran into traffic and he jumped off of an overpass. On each occasion dumb luck spared him.

This went on for some weeks before he ran into a batch mixed with fentanyl and woke up in an emergency room. Happenchance almost did what he thought had wanted to do but couldn't do himself. This time he knew this was not sustainable.

There was nobody to hold his hands and walk him to the door of the clinic. Nevertheless, he succeeded for a while and had many more months of sobriety until his next relapse.

He only used it once that time though. He returned to the clinic. It was easier this time. The tools he had gained after his first two trips seemed to sharpen with experience.

It has been almost a year since he relapsed. He still fights off overwhelming moments where his anxiety seems like the most insurmountable mountain in the world. Maybe that's the point. Not that he managed to cure himself but that he understands that he never will and yet he still fights.

You are a hero Henry. I wish you all of the strength, luck, and love in the world as you continue on your own epic journey.

Henry's story is all too common and often ends in tragedy. If you or someone you know is struggling with substance abuse, a mental health crisis, or suicidal ideation, it is important to remember that there is hope. Recovery is possible. The days might be as dark as you can bear right now and you may be struggling for some time to come but better days do exist. Please don't give up.

This is a list of resources that might help you on your journey.

Substance Abuse and Mental Health Service Administration

1-800-662 Help (4357) they can also be reached online at:

www.SAMHSA.gov

Suicide Prevention Resource Center:

Call or message: 988

LET'S TALK ABOUT IDENTITY.
THE THINGS WE CHOOSE TO SAY
AND THE THINGS WE DON'T.

The ragged people. I initially chose that term for the unhoused population of the kingdom because that was the word that was used in that world. This phrase may come off as a slur but that is not how it is intended.

People are not ragged as a state of being. Ragged is something that people run. Often by circumstances way beyond their control. One cannot blame them for looking rough when they have to do more with less just to survive.

It is worth noting that just by surviving under circumstances that would have overwhelmed so many others, they are committing a tremendous act of love. One which feeds the Kindness and starves the Terror. You have to love yourself in order to keep going when all odds are stacked against you and the systems of the world are running you ragged. Persevere and overcome.

There are other instances in the book, like when the skinhead attacks Hope. I intentionally avoided using words that sounded like slurs. That character may have been around them in all of the worlds and for other parts of the story: however, they have clung so rigidly to a misguided system of beliefs and maintained a love of intolerance that I, myself, cannot tolerate. I feel that they did not deserve to be named or to have any of their views validated in written word.

I wish I had better answers to the question of racism. It is a very real phenomenon. It is not just limited to the personal views of a narrow-minded few. There are problems with the very institutions at the heart of this country. Policies that were created for the sake of disparaging non-white people still exist. Other policies that were never intended to cause harm but still do because of historical disparities, they continue to perpetuate these inequalities.

I am not a smart enough person to feel like I could tackle this entire phenomenon by myself, though I try to do my part. There are many organizations led by smarter people than me who have put a lot more thought into the subject than myself. Some of these organizations find themselves under fire for the work that they are attempting and which has become part of a larger culture war. I am not here to say what is right or what is wrong but I do encourage everyone to look and decide for themselves how best to battle the effects of racism and inequality.

For more information you can look at:

www.naacp.org

www.blacklivesmatter.com

Sometimes the issue of racism or disparity is played out as a political issue. It is not. If you can not or will not connect to these groups, there is also a website for self-titled conservatives against discrimination located at:

www.allamericans.org

I'm not endorsing any website or their views. I don't expect anyone to adopt my opinions. All I am saying is that these sites exist with information for you to look into and find out what you agree with.

HOPE'S OTHER NAME

There is a point in this story where Hope is between identities. Hope had decided on a new identity but was not quite ready to reveal that identity to the world. The language I chose for these stages of Hope's journey were chosen out of respect for where he was in the journey.

Jasmine is of the belief that this is only the beginning of Hope's journey. That may be. At which point, when I discuss Hope, I will do so with complete respect for the identity and pronouns that Hope chooses.

Unlike the skinhead, I limited Jasmine's part in this story because her personal story is not mine to tell. Perhaps in the telling of this book, she will find her way to the appropriate author and the whole world will get to know what an insightful, funny and brilliant woman she is.

Jasmine; however, feels like her story (coming from a Cis male) might come off as a tacky patronizing.lip service that takes away from the larger story I am telling.

She was one of the more important people in this story. It was in meeting her and in Nancy's acceptance that Hope learned something about his own identity.

Hope was not traditionally a masculine name in any of the worlds he visited. Hope nonetheless, was the part of Grandmother that he found himself identifying with. Maybe one day as he gets older this will lead to other refinements of his identity. Then again, maybe it won't. Either way, I will respect it because I believe that all people should be allowed to decide how they are identified.

BIGGER THAN YOU SEE.

The Kindness and the Terror both refer to themselves as *bigger than you see*. It is hard for me to explain just how big as much of them exists in a fourth-dimensional space that we don't have access to. This space spreads across the nexuses between other universes.

They are so big, that in every fiber of our bodies, every molecule that makes us who we are and in everything we touch, their mycelium-like threads that root them to these world's can be found to exist. This is why everybody we meet has the capacity for both acts of great beauty and atrocious cruelty.

The king didn't need to invite the Terror into his world. It was already there. It had always been there. Hope didn't need to barter to allow the Kindness into the Dark World. It already existed there. The Terror; however, has a penchant for making bad deals and horrific spectacles and he used both Henesy and Hope to those ends.

A LOVE STORY?

The title of this book: *Monster Sandwiches: A Love Story.* It might lead some people to believe this was a book where two people would spend the majority of it longing for one another. It is not that sort of book. I do: however, stand behind the fact that this was indeed a love story. The king's love for his departed wife and son lead him to a dark place where he thought he could end death itself. He knew what he was doing was wrong and on some level never really believed the lies he told himself and others but by the time he realized his own mistake, it was too late.

Hope, unlike many of the other nexus keepers before him, had avoided meeting his grandmother as a child. I think he would have come to love her sooner if he had. Instead, he had issues with her and with himself because his identity didn't fit him. On his journey, he made friends that he came to love dearly and also came to terms with just what it was his grandmother was attempting to do.

In one world Sam committed an act of love by relocating a spider he had almost trodden on. In the other world, Sam crushed it with no regard for the creature. Love and the absence of love set this whole story into motion.

Throughout this book, I tried to examine the different kinds of love. Not just romantic love but the love of art. The love of self and identity, the love of community. Unselfish love and selfish love.

I didn't have any sweeping theories about love, nor did I draw any conclusions. Love isn't something that can be grasped by analysis alone. It is more than a feeling. It is also an action.

Like many other romantics, I do feel the action of love is desperately needed in this world and that it can help make the world a better place. I am not so romantic as to feel like love alone is the cure though.

The Beatles were wrong when they sang that all you need is love. We also need to be insightful and to think about the effect our actions have on others. We need food, shelter, hope and mercy. We need leaders who will not be led astray when the Terror whispers hateful things into their ears with the promise of fortune or glory. We need books, especially the kind of books that we are told not to read. We need to be afforded the autonomy to lead lives that are meaningful to us, even if other people can't understand why.

That being said, we also need love, and lots of it. Not the romantic love that you have come to expect from other love stories but the types of love I was hoping to examine. The real stuff that recognizes the autonomy, goodness, value, and importance of this entire amazing world and everyone in it.

In that way, what I am trying to say is: I love you. Don't make it creepy. Life is hard and damn terrifying sometimes. I see you. I see your struggles and the kindness you give when no one is looking. The tears you shed when you think you are alone. I see your hopelessness and the hope you find in spite of it. I see all of the good and love you for it. I see all of the bad and love you in spite of it.

I will not lie to you and promise you that everything is going to be all right or get better. I am going to tell you that it is alright and that we can try to make it better. It is worth trying.

The capacity for horror in this world is boundless but so is the capacity for love, hope, compassion, and really good bread.

A Couple More Resources

The website www.nationalhomeless.org is full of resources for people who may be experiencing or about to experience homelessness.

If you are or know of someone who is a victim of human trafficking please call the national human trafficking hotline at 1-888-373-7888.

See ya. Ok, this time I mean it. I've really got to go...

This is not the end of the story either. This was just the picture I was given. The story itself is so much bigger than we can see or understand. I am a character in it and so are you. Neither of us will ever know how it really ends or how the next picture will look but much of that depends on whether we feed Kindness or the Terror. So I will refrain from concluding this with: *the end*. I will conclude this the only way I know how. I will say that I've got to get going now, one last time. Since I have already added several extensions to our conversation, I will extend you one last goodbye and take care of yourself before going on my way.

"Goodbye. Take care of yourself."

ABOUT THE AUTHOR

Heath Eckstine lives in the northwest woods of Wisconsin with his wife of
twenty years and their three offspring that he is infinitely proud of. He has
been writing since high school but he also enjoys keeping arachnids, reptiles,
and amphibians. A lot of the character names in this story come from some of
his favorite genus and species of spider and tarantulas. He also spends a lot of
time in the outdoors running ultra marathons, biking, snowshoeing and
foraging for wild mushrooms and plants with his family.

Made in the USA
Monee, IL
28 February 2023

28538351R00142